SHWEDAGON

Noleen Jordan

ISBN: 1511461268
ISBN-13: 9781511461269
Library of Congress Control Number: 2015908140
CreateSpace Independent Publishing Platform
North Charleston, South Carolina

To my family — the only gems I could ever worship.

CONTENTS

PROLOGUE—LAND OF GOLD

Twelfth Century—Ancient Pagan

Long, broad wings extend in full flight as the great bustard hovers on the updraft. Below him are the dry plains of Pagan in upper Burma. The land closest to the river is abundant with greenery, thanks to the late-summer rains. Now, five months later, the sun is hot on his feathers, and the air is hazy in the morning light.

As the sun rises over Mount Popa in the distance, the landscape of spires comes into view. Thousands of stupas, the dome-shaped Buddhist structures also called pagodas in Asia, give a romantic view of country life in ancient Burma. The atmosphere is relaxed and soothing, with air fresh from the morning dew near the river. The sun's rays form a golden glow across the red bricks of the stupas.

There are few windbreaks. Trees are sparse in the barren area between the river to the west and the mountains to the east. Twisters send dust particles spinning into the air, eroding the soil around the growing number of buildings taking over the horizon.

Erosion is becoming a problem, with parts of the perimeter disappearing from the rectangular enclave. For the moment, the skyline retains tall toddy palms. They are joined by exotic cotton trees and bougainvilleas that bring colour but little shade to life in an arid landscape.

Squirrels scamper up the stone lions that pair up to flank the doors to the temples. Ascending tiers of the monastery roof are decorated with carved-wood fascia, reminiscent of lace.

Where wealth allows, stupas are covered with layers of gold. Temples are crowned with golden mitres studded with gems. The whole effect is to make Pagan look like a "land of gold."

The great bustard has brown upper colouring with white underneath. He has a long grey neck and head; the golden colouring on his back increases with age. These territorial birds prefer the open plains and steppes of the Old World. They look to inhabit areas with wild cereal crops and fodder plants.

He is happy with dry seeds but supplements these with insects, rodents, lizards, and frogs when he can. Being an omnivore, he is happy to settle for an area with much insect activity when his favourite plants are not available. The Ayeyarwady River in the distance and the hot sun overhead help meet this need. In the subtropics, bugs breed incessantly after the rains.

His long legs, long neck, and barrel-chested body belie his wingspan of almost two metres. At nearly seven kilograms, he prefers to stay on the ground. Here in Burma, his clan are prone to fly south in the cold season. He is forced to take flight; then he remembers that he is a strong flier. He can reach speeds of up to eighty kilometres per hour while in flight.

Beneath him the humans are hard at work. He sees the spires of the stupas they are building across the wide landscape. As he climbs higher, the scene before him unfolds to show a landscape dotted with thousands of structures. So many humans now working hard to eke out a living across this vast plain, cultivating the land and changing his habitat. The great bustards are slowly being forced out. He does not yet know that he is one of the last great bustards in Burma—his kind will soon be extinct here.

Meanwhile, among the humans, Buddhists are still building stupas, known locally as *zedis*. King Sithu I is overseeing completion of the Thatbyinnyu Temple. At a finished height of around sixty-one metres, this will be the tallest temple in Pagan.

Slow bullock carts throw up dust along the trail. Locals on horse-drawn carts drag handmade bricks to the building site. On other stupas, a layer of stucco is being added. Men, clad in the local long skirt known as a *longyi,* chew copious amounts of betel nut, spitting the juice into the dust. Women work on the lacquerware that has become famous. Overgrown weeds shelter loitering dogs.

The sheer number of *zedis* and the incredible architecture set Pagan apart. While these evolved from early Pyu design, the Pagan stupas lead the way in temple design. Each has its own distinct personality.

Masonry craftsmanship here is said to be second to none. The perfection shows in the work by local tradesmen building these monuments. Some stupas have a new pentagonal floor plan. This will allow for the inclusion of the coming of the fifth Buddha. He is destined to be replaced every five thousand years.

Some buildings support vaulted ceilings. All are built to survive the earthquakes that regularly hit the area. There are now nearly ten thousand spires. Pagan is dominated by religion.

Boys are brought by their parents to the Ananda Temple. They are to be initiated today, so that they can become monks for a time. Each lad is dressed in a sequined gown, his head adorned with flowers, his face made up. Built two hundred years before, in 1091, Ananda is Pagan's holiest temple.

A procession of monks is announced by a little bell struck by the leading monk. They walk the sandy path, parading barefoot. The eldest shepherds the youngest. The line is a show of ever-decreasing size as the youngest monks, some only three years old, bring up the rear.

The name Pagan (pronounced Bagan by the locals) is derived from the Old Burmese meaning "Pyu Village."

Pagan is the economic, political, and cultural centre of the Pagan Empire. Over the last 250 years, the rulers and their wealthiest subjects have constructed massive numbers of monuments and public buildings.

As the city prospered and grew in size, it also grew in grandeur. This is the centre of the Kingdom of Pagan, the first unification of Burma.

The king has granted a tax deduction for those donating land to build these temples. The local wealthy farmers and land owners have taken advantage of this. None of them have paid taxes in years. It doesn't hurt that they see it as highly beneficial to build a stupa to protect their karma.

The landscape has been dramatically changed forever. By the time they are finished, there will be over ten thousand Buddhist temples and pagodas erected here, as well as three thousand monasteries, libraries, and ordination halls. The whole plain of Pagan has become a site of worship and contemplation. It is truly a site to behold. There is nothing like it anywhere else in the world.

Within a hundred years, it will all start to fall apart. After repeated invasions by the Mongols to the north, the Pagan Empire collapses in AD 1287. When Marco Polo visited in the late thirteenth century, he described Pagan as a "gilded city alive with tinkling bells and the swishing sounds of monks' robes." Most of the monuments, stupas, and other buildings will fall into decay. Only those regularly visited by the locals will be maintained.

Far in the future, at the turn of the twenty-first century, only about twenty-two hundred stupas will remain. But what is being achieved here in Pagan will never be forgotten; these feats are in themselves monumental.

Far to the south, the heritage of Pagan stupas is continued in the building of the Shwedagon Pagoda in Yangon.

This is the new Land of Gold, where wealth is shown by covering a temple in real gold, and decorating it with gemstones—very large gemstones!

1

HANNAH

Hannah paid the taxi driver and picked up her large, custom-made case. She approached the gate to Commonwealth Park and showed her special access pass to gain entry. Parking close to the gate was always difficult, so a taxi today had made more sense. The bulky drone case she was carrying made it imperative.

At nearly sixty years old, Hannah Nolan's appearance belied her years, and she still had the enthusiasm of a woman half her age. Her positive attitude pushed her to continue to work while others looked down the barrel of retirement.

Indeed her husband, just a few months younger, was already talking about finishing work. Hannah knew she would be bored to tears if she gave up her business. She had spent many years building it up and still found it very fulfilling.

This was one of her favourite gigs each year. She loved coming to Floriade, especially when she got special access ahead of the official opening. It was so peaceful before the crowds arrived.

Floriade was Canberra's spring garden festival, held during the four weeks from early September to early October and finishing before the thunderstorm season started. It had proved very popular and was still going strong long after its inception as a one-time display for Australia's bicentennial celebrations in 1988, which was also the seventy-fifth birthday of the nation's capital city, Canberra.

Gardeners spent months planting more than a million tulip bulbs. These were joined by poppies, pansies, irises, hyacinths, and daffodils. The garden committee selected a different theme each year, and planting was scheduled to ensure continual blooms over the month the event would be open. The result was a feast for the eyes and senses of every member of a crowd of more than four hundred thousand visitors each year.

Hannah loved Canberra's changing seasons. While the summers were generally hot, the winters were cool, even cold by Australian standards. Winter snow fell on the ranges around Canberra but melted quickly when it fell on the plains of the capital basin. The overnight chill in the air helped make for spectacular blooms in springtime. While there had always been plenty of winter rains, Canberra also enjoyed plenty of summer sunshine.

Hannah had always thought Commonwealth Park made an ideal showcase for Canberra. It had so much going for it with its location alongside Lake Burley Griffin. Hannah loved the beautifully landscaped gardens, lovely little ponds, and interesting water features. There were bike and walking trails for those more active — something to appeal to everyone. Hannah particularly liked the sculpture of a flock of metal birds that had been retained from Floriade 1991.

From the Regatta Point end of Commonwealth Park, Hannah could see some of Canberra's landmark buildings—the National Gallery, High Court, and National Library – on the other side of the lake. The city of Canberra had been built on an area known as Sullivans Plain. Sitting between Mount Ainslie and Black Mountain, the site was selected in 1908 as the location of the new federal capital. Hannah was embarrassed to explain the origin of the city's name to visitors. Its name was believed to have come from the indigenous language, literally translating as "hollow between two breasts," as the two mountains were referred to by the aborigines. Hannah remembered reading about the city's first European owner, one Joshua Moore, who was granted title to one thousand acres at "Canberry" in 1827.

While Chicago architect Walter Burley Griffin is officially recognised as the designer of Canberra, Hannah discovered during her time at university that his wife, Marion Mahony Griffin, had worked alongside him to develop the city grid. The city plan was finally implemented in 1913. Sadly, Marion's input was barely recognised in historical narratives, but she was one of Hannah's heroes. Marion Mahony Griffin was one of the world's first women to qualify as an architect. Hannah loved her artistic watercolour drawings of famous buildings that she had designed while working with Frank Lloyd Wright. The drawing of Amberg House in Michigan and Henry Ford's proposed Dearborn Mansion (known as FairLane) were Hannah's favourites. She recalled with a sigh that the Dearborn Mansion was never built.

Hannah understood that development of Canberra had been slow. Lake Burley Griffin at the city's centre had not fully formed until nearly 50 years after Canberra was dedicated as the new capital. Hannah was surprised to find out that the lake had not been filled until 1964. She was sure this fact would surprise most Australians.

Regatta Point, on Lake Burley Griffin was a place Hannah loved to share with overseas visitors to Canberra. There was a wonderful display of the nation's history set up as a permanent exhibition. Outside on the terrace was one her favourite spots to kick back and enjoy a break, or grab a beer and a bite to eat. It was simply named "the Deck" and the scenery over the lake from here was lovely.

The park was easily accessible by car, bus, and even ferry across the lake, so it was a popular destination for Canberrans. So many activities were held in the park as a result—Australia Day festivals, marathons, weddings, concerts and even family picnics. It was a natural choice for Floriade.

The ferry ride around the lake was one of Hannah's standby activities when entertaining guests from other states or overseas. A highlight of the journey was passing the Captain Cook Memorial water jet and the Globe in the middle of the lake near Regatta Point. This landmark was an open caged globe, with the world's land masses depicted in beaten copper. Against markings of longitude and latitude, it traced Captain Cook's voyages of exploration.

The water jet spurted to a height of 147 metres. It made a spectacular sight against the backdrop of downtown Canberra on one side and Capitol Hill on the other.

As a photographer of note, Hannah had again been chosen to document the gardens of Floriade. Her images would be used for television commercials and tourism ads in magazines across the world.

It had been a warm spring, so the flowers had shot into bloom early this year. The garden beds were awash with colour. The atmosphere was one of joy, and Hannah smiled at the beauty all around her.

Her photographer's eye was drawn to beds of simple white flowers with centre spots of vibrant-purple plantings and to multitudes of colourful poppies intertwined with masses of tulips in every imaginable colour.

Hannah walked past the retail stalls where vendors would be shouting their wares tomorrow. She continued down the hill past the Ferris wheel in the amusement park section. She was in awe at the abundance of flowers in the gardens this year, soaking in the colours and designs on her way down the hill.

Cherry blossoms were abundant—the light breeze shed the blooms like pink snow onto the paths below.

Tomorrow the place would be packed with families climbing around garden beds, eating gourmet snack foods, and riding the Ferris wheel. Café Valenti would be packed with those weary from walking for hours around the garden beds, jostled by others who were just looking to cool off in the warm spring weather.

Hannah found her "centre spot" in the middle of the floral displays, close to the gardening students' beds, with their scarecrows dressed to delight. From here she could look down over the largest pond. Trees provided shade along the shore, enticing picnickers. Weeping willows were back in leaf, their long tendril branches kissing the ground and licking the water at the edge of the pond. Hannah lifted her case onto a park bench; the case was bulky but not overly heavy.

For this job, she was using her favourite Canon 5D EOS camera and her smaller drone. Her hexacoptor of choice was the Versadrone X6 Mk II. She had ordered it custom built with a full carbon-fibre frame and a moulded carbon-fibre fuselage. It was known to be incredibly easy to transport and easy to put together almost anywhere. So it should be, given its price.

The case clicked open, and Hannah unpacked her drone for the first aerial shots. Selecting the various component parts from their foam cut-outs, she assembled the drone in less than two minutes, easily clicking the pieces together.

This was an expensive piece of kit, even for a professional photographer, but Hannah thought it was worth every penny it cost to customize it for her own camera. She was quite tech-savvy where cameras and their accoutrements were concerned, and she loved the in-flight stability of the drone and its advanced flight-control systems.

Hannah inserted the lithium-polymer flight batteries and checked the AV downlink with the LCD screen fitted to the Futaba 14SQ transmitter. She clicked the Canon into the high-precision brushless camera mount and selected the "failsafe return to base" function. She pulled out her iPad, already programmed to drive the drone. She tested the transmitter and used the semi-automatic take-off feature to get the drone in the air within minutes. In the sky above her, the drone looked like a black scorpion as Hannah unfolded the drone's three massive, spiky claws. She realised it looked like it might attack with its six sharp-looking propellers paired on the top of each claw.

The drone was very quiet overhead, with its low-profile, high-efficiency brushless motors. The first-person-view glasses let Hannah see exactly what the drone was seeing. She knew its range would be enough to cover the entire Floriade field.

Hannah shot for nearly fifteen minutes before bringing the drone back to replace the batteries for extra flying time. She was glad she had invested in the extra batteries. After some forty minutes of flying time, the drone had moved around all the garden beds to capture every aspect of the floral display, as well as the entertainment stages, exhibition booths, and restaurants within the park. Hannah quickly reviewed her shots on the camera's screen. She had everything she needed—the shoot was done.

Now she could relax a little and enjoy the atmosphere of the park. The area was quiet before the gates opened to the public the next day—a far cry from her last official visit here for a commercial shoot on Australia Day. When the fireworks started at day's end, the evening sky filled with over six thousand bats alarmed by the sudden noise.

The local bat population had been growing in numbers for some years. The colony of fruit bats had exploded after the bushfires on the south coast of New South Wales, an hour away. With little food left on the trees there, the bats had migrated to Canberra's cooler climes in vast numbers, to sample its blossoms and berries. They were now so cosy that they had never left. Even after the fireworks, they were back within an hour. Hannah had managed some amazing photos of them in flight on that occasion.

In the process of packing up her kit, she was disturbed by the ringing of her mobile phone. The screen showed the image of her husband, Simon.

"Hey, babe," she answered with a smile. Even after nearly thirty-five years, she could honestly say she was still happy to be married to this man. "What are you up to?"

"Just wondering if you are up to a little overseas jaunt," Simon said, in a teasing voice.

"Well, you've got my attention. Where were you thinking?" Hannah asked, chuckling. This was a familiar scenario.

"Myanmar," Simon responded.

"Where?" Hannah didn't immediately recognize the name.

"You might know it as Burma," Simon teased.

"OK, now I know where you mean. Didn't remember it had changed its name! When were you thinking of going, and why Burma?" Hannah was rarely surprised at Simon's sense of adventure. It had taken them to some strange places over the years, the last one being Antarctica—a photographer's paradise, as it turned out.

"Just seen an ad in today's travel section for a cruise to Burma — Myanmar, that is, at least since the late eighties, I think." Simon was an avid reader of travel sections and brochures. This proved to be an expensive addiction. Anything that involved a cruise was high on his list of perfect holiday getaways. "Ridiculously cheap, and it's a really good cruise line. What do you think? Oh, it's in December, by the way, but before Christmas. We would be home in time for the family dinner on the twenty-fifth. Can you reshuffle your commitments?"

"Yeah, I guess." Hannah was trying to remember what she had coming up. "Do we need visas?"

"For this one, yes, but the embassy is here in Canberra, so that's a no-brainer." Simon was always confident, even though he knew it would be Hannah who got to do the running around. "We can even add on a side trip to the Taj Mahal, if you like, because the cruise starts in India."

"Gotta love that! Sounds amazing. So I guess we are going to Myanmar, then. How long are we there for? " Hannah was shaking her head — never a dull moment in her life with Simon.

"Couple of days, so plenty of time to take photos." He was cajoling her now.

"Would you send me the itinerary, please?" Hannah asked. "Might have time to set up a team tutorial excursion with the Camera Club. Nothing like having a holiday as a tax deduction!"

For some years, Hannah had been running courses as part of her photography business. There was a dedicated group of amateurs who wanted to learn how to use their cameras and understand lighting, camera angles, and exposure. The club members loved a good excuse to travel to a new destination, foreign or local, to get some different shots. Many of them were retirees, so short notice was seldom a problem. Plenty of them were from overseas and had been attracted to her online courses. They followed up by joining in some destination travel courses, as well. Most of them sold their work as stock photos, and this would often pay for their travel.

Hannah's smartphone pinged as Simon's e-mail arrived with the itinerary attached. She scanned it quickly before forwarding the e-mail to the Camera Club to find out how many might be interested in joining the cruise. There were only a few who would travel, Hannah knew. The club members who liked to travel were well acquainted with each other, having shared previous journeys and had developed lasting friendships.

When the "empty nest" had hit Hannah's life some years ago, she had thrown herself back into her photography business. It had been a part-time venture while the children were at home, but now she could make it her priority.

Her business had been a nice fall-back when the kids eventually left home to start their own lives. And the extra income had come in handy to support Simon's addiction to travel, though Hannah was now just as addicted as her husband. She loved to travel and loved the photographic opportunities it gave her.

Marriage to a detective had meant waiting for Simon through night shifts and callouts. Photography had begun as a good way to fill the hours when he was away and had become a passion.

Over the years, Hannah had earned a reputation for producing high-quality shots and being easy to work with. She had eventually moved into real-estate photography, beginning with friends who had asked her to help market their properties. Her business grew to include clients of all kinds. She had been invited into some amazing homes over the years, and the real-estate work had developed into lifestyle shots of homes of the wealthy, which were often used by magazines. Her work became well known and highly appreciated. Recently, the drones had made it possible for her to get the best external aspects and even take full 360-degree aerial shots of any property.

She was surprised when an old schoolmate had contacted her out of the blue. He asked her to help with a special project for the government. She had no idea that he worked for ASIO, the Australian Security and Intelligence Organisation. He was involved in the espionage squad.

Hannah didn't believe him at first. It took a few phone calls and a face-to-face meeting at the ASIO headquarters in Canberra to convince her that he was indeed a government agent working on high-level secret inquiries.

It took even longer to persuade Hannah to get involved. They were convinced that she was perfect for the role. Her high profile meant she would be accepted into any social event to mingle with any crowd. Her age made her less of a suspect. For the first time, being older proved to be an advantage!

Hannah had eventually been convinced that this work would be supporting Simon's police work, helping the government to stop crime. She signed a document to ensure she told no-one, not even her husband.

At first, it was just taking photos through open windows of cars and homes. *Harmless enough*, thought Hannah. Over the years, the gigs became more intimate, and she found herself guiding the drone through open windows of offices and hotels and even into specific rooms. Occasionally, she even happened to be invited into a home or embassy office for a legitimate location shoot, which she used as reconnaissance.

Sometimes she included photos of what was on a desk. If there was something she couldn't photograph in place, she would find a way to return later on and remove it. The engineering team at ASIO had designed a computerised hook with a basket to hang beneath the drone. This allowed Hannah to pass the item to ASIO. They would keep it for a very short time, and then Hannah would return it to its original position. This required exact positioning, based on photos she had shot before the item was removed.

It wasn't long before ASIO had her accessing keys, mobile phones, and even documents and diaries from desks, bedside chests, and hall tables. Embassies, hotel rooms, and private homes around Canberra were all targets.

Hannah was called on day and night, so now Simon's shift work was working in her favour, helping to cover her extracurricular activities. Simon had no idea Hannah was involved with any of this. If he came home unexpectedly, would he suspect her of having an affair? Probably not, given that Simon was neither suspicious nor jealous. If he had found out about the ASIO work, he would have conceded that she was doing important work for the government. Hannah was uncomfortable telling him though, so it stayed a secret, thanks to the document she had signed. It still felt "dirty" to Hannah.

While Hannah wasn't comfortable with the "project work" at first, she liked the extra income. Working for ASIO paid generously. Her photography business was doing well, but it was still nice to have some "cushion" in the bank account.

She was terrified in the beginning, but soon the adrenaline became a welcome rush. She started to miss the adrenaline adventure between jobs for ASIO.

That's why she went out on her own. All those jewels lying around in homes and hotels, little gold statuettes sitting on desks in embassies, expensive watches left on bedside tables while their owner stepped into the shower. Hannah knew she could take them, ASIO had taught her that. She was careful not to mix her personal jobs with the ASIO work.

There was a time when she had felt really guilty about it. She had known it would end badly if Simon ever found out. Her husband was as honest as they get, so her own activities placed her ethics well below Simon's. She loved him to bits, but she still couldn't help herself when it came to stealing. She had become addicted to the adrenaline rush. The challenge, the heist, the reward, were all too tempting. Hannah knew the risks.

It was an interesting conundrum, being married to a detective while becoming a thief. Simon had told her many stories over the years about catching criminals, so at least she knew how to cover her tracks. She also knew how ASIO worked and how to avoid detection. They were not used to looking in their own backyard, but why risk it?

Hannah instinctively knew that it would not be smart to work in her own territory. When pocketing things that belonged to other people, it made sense to take her work overseas. Holidays gave her the perfect opportunity. Being a photographer was a great cover: she could always decide to take some night shots while her hubby retired to bed.

Her biggest problem was hiding the income from her beloved husband. With her own photography business, she could easily overstate her profits in the short term. Simon was not one to get involved in the accounting side of her business.

It was when she started earning millions that her second life became harder to hide. She had opened a bank account on a trip to Switzerland some years ago and had stashed the proceeds of her crimes there ever since. But it wasn't really about the money.

She loved the thrill of planning her next crime and then putting that plan into play. It was quite amusing, really, because Hannah was not interested in jewellery, or any kind of "bling." She no longer even wore her wedding ring. When questioned, she would tell people that it was because she was twice the woman Simon had married, a reference to midlife weight gain.

Actually, she wasn't what you would call a "girly girl." She wasn't into having her nails done at a salon or shopping for endless pairs of shoes. Always well dressed, she presented well, with an air of confidence about her. She certainly did not look like a thief!

She did like a challenge, though.

Hannah's problem was that she was smart. At just twelve years of age, she had been offered membership to Mensa, the international organization for people whose IQ was in the ninety-eighth percentile or higher. A standard school IQ test showed her to be well ahead of anyone else her age. Up until then she did not know she was smarter than anyone else. She just figured she found things easier to learn than others did. At twelve, nobody gave these things much thought.

As she got older, she realised she had the ability to break things down in order to explain them to others. This was when she learned how to teach. She found she had lots of patience for teaching highly technical camera settings to ordinary folks.

When traveling, she would often take a group of amateur photographers with her as a cover for her escapades. After all, who was going to question a motley group of camera geeks on a photographic excursion?

Her little misdemeanours had grown in size since the early days, and she was now into some serious stuff. Her contacts list was extensive. Her ability as a photographer had opened a lot of doors to some exclusive people and opportunities. She had no problem getting rid of the trappings from her exploits.

Burma, huh? Home to the Shwedagon Diamond. This could be interesting, she thought as she closed her case and called a taxi to take her home. She could think it through while she reviewed the day's shots back in her studio.

2

CHENNAI

Lake Chembarambakkam came into view as the Air India plane circled Chennai. The approach from the west lined them up for immediate landing.

The plane was an hour late arriving into Chennai International Airport. Even with a transfer booked, it would be a mad dash across the city to make the cruise check-in on time. It was two thirty in the afternoon when the plane came in to land. It would take another five minutes to taxi to the terminal. Hannah hoped the car service would be on time and already waiting for them; otherwise they risked missing the ship.

When Hannah had made the reservations, she had been told that (for some unknown reason) the port gates were locked at 4:30 p.m., so check-in closed at 3:30 p.m. The vessel would leave at 5:00 p.m. and would wait for no one. If only the travel agent had thought to reconfirm the departure time of the flight. It had been changed since the original booking.

Their earlier flight had been dropped and the later one brought forward, but it still left an hour's discrepancy from the original travel plan. The issued ticket even had the original time printed on it; Hannah and Simon hadn't known about the change until they checked in at the airport.

Simon grabbed the camera gear from Hannah as they prepared to deplane. "Geez, we are late! Get ready to hoof it, love!"

"I hope I have all the right paperwork for the drones" Hannah said. "If they want to see it all now, we will never make the ship"

Thankfully, their arrival gate was close to the baggage-claim area, so it wasn't far to stride. They didn't have to pace up and down for too long at Carousel Three because their luggage came off early. They each grabbed a suitcase, snapped the handle up, and righted the bags onto their wheels.

"Which way?" asked Hannah nervously.

"Follow the arrows, hon. Everybody seems to be going the same way." Simon was nearly running.

Hannah suddenly realised they had exited the Customs Hall without being questioned. The drone cases were heavy in their hands but Simon had been so focussed he had just charged straight out the door, and nobody had challenged him. *Thank Heavens,* she thought.

"Look there," barked Hannah, pointing in front of Simon. "Our name's on that sign." They closed the distance to the hired driver as Hannah called, "Hi, we are the Nolans."

"Welcome to Chennai." He was in his forties, well-groomed and well spoken, his dark skin confirming they were in sun-soaked Chennai. "My name is Arvyi. If you will follow me please, the vehicle is not far. It had to be left in the transit area. It will just take us a minute's walk, if you don't mind. We understand the urgency, Mrs. Nolan, and will do everything we can to get you safely to the ship on time. It is usually a ninety-minute drive to the port, so we pray the traffic is light."

The heat hit them as they exited the air-conditioned terminal but they ignored it to keep moving. The parking lot was in sight.

Hannah's heart sank. "Ninety minutes! But it's already two fifty. We're going to miss check-in, and they won't wait for us."

"Then we better get moving." Simon grabbed her arm and guided her toward the vehicle as the driver opened the car door. He almost pushed her into the backseat, handed her the camera case, and then slid in next to her. Arvyi finished loading the cases into the trunk and then closed the back door for them.

Arvyi pulled into the exiting traffic, paid the parking ticket at the booth, and pushed ahead toward downtown Chennai before heading for the port.

Hannah looked out at the vast city of Chennai, re-calling that it used to be called Madras. The city sat on the Coromandel Coast off the Bay of Bengal. She had heard it called the "gateway to southern India" be-cause of its location on the south eastern coast of the flat Eastern Coastal Plains.

With eight million people across the metropolis, the traffic was chaotic, but the motorway was surpris-ingly modern. Arvyi deftly manoeuvred the vehicle onto the highway and through the myriad of cars, trucks, motorbikes, and tuk-tuks.

"Tuk-tuks are not allowed in the airport precinct," he told them. "They are too dangerous."

"Why is that?" Simon asked.

"Tuk-tuks only turn three ways. They turn left, they turn right, and they turn over!" Arvyi laughed at this old joke. He tried to distract them with a little local insight. "Chennai is known as the 'Detroit of India' be-cause we have a large auto industry here, which most foreigners don't know. We are the fourth-largest city in India and the largest in Tamil Nadu," he said proudly.

"Aha." Simon was watching the clock and the traffic nervously. "When was the name changed from Madras?"

"Oh, that was some years ago now, back in 1996. Madras was the name the British gave to the lit-tle fishing village near Fort St Gorge that we call Madraspattinam. We think the Tamil word for 'face' better reflects our respect for the temples, so we re-verted to the Tamil word *chenni*."

Looking out the car window, Hannah noticed the architecture of the city was a mix of British Colonial and a modern European influence. It was surprisingly up-to-date in parts, with high-rises popping out of old suburbia. Hannah raised her camera and clicked off shots at a rate of knots.

This was not the India they had expected. They knew it was an "emerging market" but still thought that meant "third world." The expected shanty towns slipped into view every now and then — distressing but expected. What was unexpected were all the new offices and apartment blocks. The overall effect was of order and stability.

Hannah took in the colours on the streets, with every woman she saw wearing the traditional sari. The streets practically vibrated with the hot pinks, lime greens, yellows, and blues embroidered with silver or gold thread. *Just beautiful*, she thought.

School children dressed neatly in various school uniforms were already on their way home. Vendors continued to sweep around their little stalls — the streets were surprisingly clean. The fresh fruit and vegetables in the stalls look inviting. Flower stalls were still doing a roaring trade as locals bought strings of blooms as offerings for the temple.

The parks were green and well-tended, with flower beds in bloom even in the winter months. Boys played cricket wherever there was open space. Cows lay in the middle of the streets; donkeys pulled carts loaded with bricks headed for building sites. It was an amazing mix of ancient culture and modern civilisation.

They passed Tamil temples, with their rainbow-coloured fronts depicting gods and folklore. Hannah marvelled at the government buildings boasting deep-scarlet paint with white domed roofs typical of the British Colonial "Raj" era and compared these to the plain Christian churches painted simply in white, So much to take in — Hannah wasn't sure what she wanted her digital "film" to capture first.

Arvyi had managed to bring them within sight of the cranes at the industrial cargo port, so they knew they were getting close. They were disappointed to learn the passenger terminal was at a different port, some distance away yet. It was already 4:15 p.m. They had done well so far, but the pressure was still on.

"How much farther?" Simon was increasingly nervous.

"About twenty minutes, Mr. Nolan," Arvyi said as Simon groaned in despair.

They were close to Fort St George. Arvyi had a choice between two possible routes over the Cooum River. He chose Kamarajar Promenade, the road closest to the waterline around the old Fort. The traffic here was relatively light for the time of day, and they made good headway, with just over two kilometres to go to reach the port gates.

They slowed for a bus that pulled in front of them from a side street on their left and then almost limped to the next roundabout.

They slid through the open port gates. The bus stopped in front of them, apparently carrying passengers for the ship.

Immigration officials appeared, and while two of them boarded the bus to inspect passports and visa stamps, a lone officer approached the Nolans' car.

The process was swift, with only two passengers in the vehicle, and he quickly waved them on. As they pulled around the bus, they could see the ship.

"Nearly there," Simon said, finally smiling.

"Oh, God!" Hannah responded, not quite believing it. "We still have to get through check-in, *if* they are still open! It's bang on four thirty, and check-in closed an hour ago."

The car pulled onto the pier and came to a stop in front of a very antiquated shed that appeared to be abandoned.

"Come on, old girl. They haven't pulled the gangway up yet, and they have a busload of people behind us. Surely we are good to go." Hannah suspected that Simon's comments were more a prayer than a statement.

Arvyi jumped out and rapidly unloaded the suitcases. Simon thanked him with a generous handshake and an even more generous tip.

Grabbing suitcases and camera bags plus laptop and handbag, they surged into the shed, under the sign that read "Customs and Immigration."

Inside, there were forms to fill out, x-ray machines for luggage, and plenty of officials threatening to slow the process. India is renowned for bureaucracy.

There was a small line ahead of them, but at least they had arrived. Hannah started to relax.

For the first time, she realised she was being separated from Simon. Local officials herded the women into a separate line from the men. The female line involved stepping behind a curtained area for a female officer to do a pat down of one's body. Hannah wondered if anybody ever dared pat down the officer in return. She chuckled to herself at the mental image of this unlikely event.

As she approached the security line, she was asked to lift her camera cases onto the table for inspection. As always, the camera cases drew attention. She opened each case with a flourish, knowing the reaction she would get from those nearby. Their contents always drew comment, and she knew how intriguing these were for those who had not seen them previously. Hannah was questioned as to the contents of the cases and the need for them. She handed over the folder with all the documents needed to bring the drones through India, along with her business card. Hannah had made sure these were accompanied by a sweet smile and a short explanation. The officials spent ages inspecting the documents. Hannah had suspected they did not know what to do with the paperwork. *They will get filed in the bin as usual* she thought. Finally they had accepted her explanation and her luggage. She stepped out of the women-only line to re-join her husband, as the luggage was whisked away to the ship.

It was only then that they were told to proceed to the gangway to board the ship. Check-in had been moved inside due to the lateness of the hour, and the heat in the shed.

"Thank God!" Hannah whispered to Simon.

They had never been so glad to walk up a gangway as they were today. They smiled at each other, as Simon said with a sigh, "I'm getting too old for this shit!" and they entered the vessel they had longed for all afternoon.

Aptly named the *Quest*, it was a smaller vessel than they were used to sailing on. Carrying only 750 passengers at most, the atmosphere was more like that of a well-appointed home.

After reviewing the website, Hannah already knew that with seven restaurants, cafes, and lounges, plus two pools, the sun decks, and a spa, there was every chance that they would not get anywhere near the gym or the jogging track.

The *Quest* was capable of eighteen knots an hour, so it would be a sedate journey across the Andaman Sea. Hannah prayed for calm seas, as she still occasionally got queasy in large swells. Simon, on the other hand, should have been born a sailor; he never got seasick, no matter how rough the seas.

They were stopped at the top of the gangway where cool drinks were handed to them. Then they were ushered along to the Club Lounge for check-in. Most of the necessary information had already been provided online, so the process was fairly painless and (thankfully) short. They had arrived.

They turned in their passports, had their ID photos taken, and received their on-board charge cards that doubled as room keys. It was now five thirty, and clearly the ship was delayed well past its original departure time.

"Simon, do you mind if I drop the camera case in our cabin and just take the camera up on deck for departure? Plus, I need a cool drink." Hannah was emotionally exhausted after the long race to the port.

"Right you are," he agreed, "but drinks are included on this ship, so I vote for the bar on pool deck for a cold beer."

Cabin 6157 was an inside cabin amidships, or as Simon was known to say, a "coffin with a light." They had cruised so many times that they had come to realise that you got the same cruise — and the same meals and entertainment — whether you paid for the cheap seats or the expensive ones. And, as far as Simon knew, they couldn't afford the expensive ones.

They were also smart enough to know that on this cruise through the tropics, the heat was kept out of an inside cabin. Some of the balcony cabins, with their glass balcony doors, would absorb a good deal of heat.

Hannah planned to enjoy the darkness of the inside cabin to catch up on some long overdue sleep.

The cabin proved to be more than acceptable. They dumped their things, unloaded wallets, laptops, and mobile phones into the cabin safe, and headed upstairs to find the bar.

The decks were surprisingly quiet, with few people outside for departure. They suspected the heat was to blame. The band had started up in the background, and Simon, now happy with an icy beer in hand, returned from the bar. "Apparently there are only five hundred and fifty people on board. That explains the huge discount on the fares. They had to fill the ship." Amazing how much information you could get from the barman.

From the upper deck, they looked out over the port, across to the local railway station, and wondered what life was like for the locals.

"Well, we didn't get to see much of Chennai!" Hannah said with a laugh as the ship's horn sounded their departure. By the time the city had faded into the distance, Simon was on his third beer.

Hannah was grateful that evenings on board would all be "dressy casual" as there were no formal nights scheduled on this cruise. That saved packing the good gear and lugging it half way across the world. By the time they returned to their cabin, the suitcases had been delivered. They took quick showers and donned fresh clothes for dinner.

They were greeted at the restaurant door by the assistant maître d', and swiftly ushered to a table. Tonight would be a quiet dinner for two. The menu looked delicious and Simon chose a New York steak, while Hannah tried the Madras curry. She felt the need to at least sample something of the Chennai region.

They were quickly at ease, and it wasn't long before Simon commented on how pleasant the staff were. "They're a cheery lot, aren't they? Can't remember ever noticing happy staff before."

"It's because their tips have already been paid," Hannah announces. "Remember?"

They both chuckled. Australians were not known for tipping, preferring to only tip if they received exceptional service or if they received something they hadn't expected. To tip as a matter of expectation, even when service was poor, went against the grain for most Australians at home or overseas.

"There is a show after dinner, if you're interested, love," Simon said.

"Sure, why not? As long as we're still awake." Hannah knew Simon would be snoring within the hour.

3

ANDAMAN

Hannah had rolled over in bed, suddenly awake to the sounds of Simon's gentle rhythmic snoring. She looked lovingly at her husband's form, as her eyes adjusted to wakefulness. His presence always brought a smile to her face.

They had been together since their early twenties, Hannah remembered. Her first sight of this gentle man had been alluring. His toned body and his dark good looks, had been immediately captivating to her. His police uniform had been both irresistible and jarring all at once.

Her best friend had been knocked down in a hit and run accident, while crossing the road. Hannah shuddered as she remembered the event. The scream that pierced the air, the thud as the vehicle threw her friend skyward, the crashing glass that had broken beneath her friend's weight against the windscreen. It was all imprinted permanently in Hannah's memory.

The ambulance had arrived then the Police car, and out stepped Simon. She remembered how relieved she was to see a policeman yet how wretched that it was due to the events of that evening. Hannah would never understand how an horrific event for her friend, could have translated into the start of something wonderful for her and Simon. He had spoken to her at length after the ambulance had left, even taking her to the hospital to be with her friend.

Simon had returned the next morning to check up on the friend as a pretence to see Hannah again, she realised later. He had bought her a coffee in the hospital cafeteria. *Probably the worst coffee in my life,* she thought. They were married six months later; her best friend was back on her feet and walking ahead of her down the aisle as her bridesmaid.

Hannah's thoughts were brought back as Simon rolled over in bed. Hannah had swung her feet onto the floor, dressed quietly and snuck out of the cabin. Simon would sleep for hours yet.

Always an early riser, Hannah was soon on deck with coffee in hand, her camera swinging around her neck. The early morning breeze felt pleasant on her face. The Andaman Sea was under grey cloud as dawn arrived.

She looked over the ocean, hoping to find a blue whale, known to frequent this part of the world. Hannah was disappointed at how little visible life there seemed to be in the water alongside the ship — no dolphins, no flying fish.

The ocean was relatively calm with a slight swell. Hannah stood at the stern and watched the approach of a tropical storm on the horizon for over half an hour. She noticed choppy water about four hundred metres away. As it caught her eye, she realized a water spout was forming. She watched in awe as the spout grew to about fifty metres across. Disappointed that Simon was not with her to witness this natural phenomenon, she raised her camera and started clicking away, frame after frame. She was thankful for her camera — she could still show him what he had missed out on.

Hannah's thoughts had again turned to Simon. She knew what he would make of her escapades. *A bit like the storm brewing out there,* she thought. She had always known her husband had strong ethics. *Simon is straight down the line,* Hannah mused. If he ever found out that his wife had been stealing, he would divorce her. She had shuddered then, the hairs on her arms lifted in response to the thought. She knew he would never be able to forgive her for the subterfuge. *Sorry darling, I just can't help myself. It is way too much fun,* Hannah pondered.

After an hour on deck, capturing photos of the sunrise, the sea, and the sky, Hannah grabbed a coffee and early morning pastry from the café. They were gone before she got back to the cabin to rouse Simon for breakfast.

They always preferred the dining room for breakfast rather than room service. One of the things they both loved about cruising was being served breakfast. It always felt like a Sunday morning outing when the silver service came out early in the day. They were surrounded by choices: tropical fruits and yoghurts, bacon and eggs with all the trimmings (for Simon), eggs Benedict with its velvety Hollandaise sauce oozing down the sides of the eggs (for Hannah). Of course, wherever the ship was located meant local delicacies at meals, as well. Breakfast was no different. In Asia, you could expect rice, vegetables, and tofu, so it was not surprising to find some curries on the morning menu here in the Bay of Bengal.

"Hannah!" called a voice from a nearby table. Molly Johns, a member of the Camera Club, was waving her handkerchief in the air.

Hannah smiled and excused herself from Simon, as she walked over to Molly's table

"Molly. Hi, glad to see you looking so well!" Hannah smiled a greeting at Molly's table companions.

"Takes a lot to keep this old girl down," Molly said, laughing. At sixty-eight, she was surprisingly agile and her slender physique showed she stayed in good shape. Molly was typical of British-born emigrants to Perth in Western Australia: well-tanned, distinctive strawberry-blonde hair, and the elegant accent of a true Pom. "I flew in a couple of days early to enjoy Chennai. Figured I wasn't likely to get back here in a hurry."

"I wish we had done the same." Hannah sighed gently, remembering yesterday's dash to the port. "Hope you've got some great shots to show me."

"Thrilled with what I have captured! Chennai is amazing. Even got to see them filming a movie; apparently, this area is the capital of the Tamil film industry—they call it Kollywood, not Bollywood!" Molly said. "Even got out of town to Pondicherry on the south coast. Great beach and brilliant ice cream!"

"Sounds gorgeous. Can't wait to see the pics." Hannah was genuinely enthusiastic, as she loved to see their work. "If you'll excuse me, Molly, I best get back to hubby. Are you coming to the meet-and-greet?"

"Absolutely. See you there." Molly waved hello to Simon, who was now making gestures to his wife.

After their long, leisurely breakfast, they found the grey skies had blown away and the sun was now shining. Simon and Hannah decided on a morning in a sun chair with plenty of sunscreen. Hannah was reading when a shadow fell over her.

"Well, what have we here?" Jock McAdams, at age seventy-five, was a retired Scottish hotelier who travelled with his partner, Gordon. "If I were in a Camera Club, I would be taking photos of this gorgeous lady."

Hannah sat up and reached for her sun wrap. "Don't you dare, Jock! Some things are off-limits!"

"Oh, but they would make such nice blackmail shots," Jock said, laughing. "See you at the soiree this afternoon, Miss Hannah." He smiled as he walked away.

"If he weren't gay, I would be jealous of his attentions to you," Simon joked.

For Hannah, the one problem with being on a ship was that it was almost impossible not to run into someone she knew. When she was the one who had organized a private tour group of people, the odds were multiplied.

"*Well,*" Hannah told herself, "*if I didn't like these people, they would not have been invited to join the club!* "

Lunch was a lazy affair by the pool, with Buffalo wings and burgers, washed down with an icy cold beer for Simon, who was in his element.

At a quarter to three, Simon and Hannah, showered and freshly dressed, sauntered into the *Quest's* drawing room. Hannah always arranged a get-together for the Camera Club, both as a welcoming gesture, and as an information and Q and A session. Today she had opted for a three o'clock afternoon tea, always a treat on a cruise liner.

Staff members were adding the finishing touches, having ensured the room was fully set up with a variety of teas and coffee. The room had a lovely ambience with its rich wood panelling with dark carpets and dark furniture. The lighting was subdued and mirrors reflected the muted lighting across the room. The curtains had been pulled back to allow afternoon light to wash across the library shelves and lighten the mood.

Small tables covered with crisp white linen and silver cutlery had been placed around the room. Trays of tea sandwiches, scones, and petits fours adorned each table. Staff hovered discreetly in the background. The room felt elegant and refined.

Simon played host in order to allow Hannah to greet her club members and generally work the room. The first to arrive were the American "twitchers" — birdwatchers dedicated to finding rare species. Hilary and Aaron Swanston, who had been building their birdlife lists since their teens, had plenty of experience in chasing prized rare birds around North America. They had joined Hannah's club as a way of exploring farther afield and improving their camera skills.

Aaron was a dentist and his wife worked as his dental technician. Tall and nerdy looking, Aaron was balding, making him look older than his fifty-four years. His mousey brunette wife was short and fidgety, and clearly in charge of organising their lives. While he seemed boring, she seemed bored.

"Hello, you two. Haven't seen you since Japan last year. How's the family?" Hannah kept notes on her club members and ensured she knew the names of children, pets, home towns, etc. just for such moments.

"Well, thank you, Hannah." Hilary was quick to jump in.

"We hope to find some Nicobar pigeons, you know," Aaron interjected. "Only found on Andaman and Nicobar islands. Oh, and Myanmar, of course.

They have amazing green feathers on their back that reflect the colours of the rainbow. Well, so we're told. Haven't seen one yet."

"We'll do what we can, Aaron." Hannah was reassuring. "Please help yourself to some tea, and I'll catch up with you shortly."

Ted and Laura Glenn stepped out of the elevator. "Simon dear, so good to see you again." Laura kissed Simon on the cheek.

"And you, Laura." Simon turned to take Ted's hand. "Ted, how are you, mate?"

"Really well, thanks, Simon. Glad to be away, to be honest! Retirement is not all it's cracked up to be, you know." Ted always showed signs of retirement boredom. He had been a court clerk for over forty years before retiring two years ago. He and Simon often swapped stories of criminals and how they got caught. "I'm looking forward to the trip. Always enjoy Hannah's jaunts."

A young couple approached the door. "Hannah" called Nathan Donaldson. He and his new bride Amanda were the youngest recruits to the Camera Club. They had eloped just before leaving their home town of Portsmouth in England. The opportunity to make the cruise their honeymoon was too good to pass up.

Nathan had come to the club in a round- about way. His late mother, Deidre, was a long time member of the club, and had introduced Nathan to it five years ago. He had initially accompanied his dear old mum, and had then stayed on after she passed away. Hannah had been pleased to hear that Nathan had married, even though his bride had no interest in cameras. *Just like Simon,* Hannah thought.

"Nathan. Welcome and Congratulations to you both." Hannah kissed him on the cheek and then turned to his wife. "Amanda. Lovely to have you with us. It is so good to meet you. Please let me introduce you to some of our members — the others will be here shortly. We are quite a diverse group, as Nathan explained, so I'm sure you will fit right in." She drew the Donaldsons into the room and made the appropriate introductions. Hannah knew the Glenns would be hospitable and engaging. She hoped the Swanstons wouldn't prove too boring for the newlyweds.

The others arrived in due course, and soon the room was abuzz with conversation and laughter. They were a happy lot when they got together. Their shared interest in cameras and photography soon brought them out of themselves.

Amanda had to learn names to attach to faces. The only thing she knew about the individuals so far was that they shared a common interest in photography, all except Simon.

"So what does Simon do?" she had asked Nathan.

"He's a detective, a fingerprint expert actually." Nathan had told her.

Ted chimed in to the conversation "He's a very good fingerprint expert with over twenty years of experience. In fact it was his team that developed the world's first treatment that allowed a fingerprint to be lifted from human skin. Usually they can only lift prints off flat surfaces, you know, doors, windows and so on, so getting a print off a dead body for example was impossible, before his team figured out how to do it. It's helped solved murders all over the world since then."

"Wow, how interesting" Amanda was impressed.

"But he's also human" Hannah had joined them. "He'll tell you himself about driving a police car in the early days. He was on duty when he came across a Police radar speed trap unit on the roadside. As soon as he saw the other police car, he hit the brakes, worrying that he might be driving too fast. As he slid past the other coppers, they waved to him, and that's when he remembered he was in uniform and driving a police car." They all laughed.

"The funny thing is" Hannah had to explain "that he uses a very powerful camera at work to photograph fingerprints. But by the time he gets home the last thing he wants to do is use a camera. Go figure."

Hannah overheard Simon telling Digby the tale of trying to get visas from the Myanmar Embassy. "Wasn't that a laugh?" Simon said sarcastically. "Hannah finally found the embassy. She didn't want to trust our passports to the post, and when she got there, she found boxes piled high all around the office walls. With two women working away squeezed between the boxes, the place looking like it was packed up waiting for the removalists. So Hannah says to them 'Oh, are you moving?' And the bird says, 'No, it always looks like this.' Hannah didn't know what to think."

"Not to mention the paperwork I had to fill in for the drones" Hannah had joined them. "I thought I would be the one moving in!" she sighed. The men laughed.

Tea was served. A hush fell over the room as they all stuffed their faces with goodies from the tea trays.

Hannah took the opportunity to make a short speech. "If I can have your attention for a few moments, please? I just want to go through some of the vital bits of information for the coming days. First, welcome to you all, and thank you for coming. We are in for quite an adventure. I have sent to your cabins all the information you need for the upcoming ports of call. Each one has its own excursions for you to choose from, according to your preferences. Please let me know which ones you choose, because I cannot be on all of them. I will give you whatever pointers you need before you join your day trip. Just let me know what you hope to capture, if there is anything special on your list.

"Our first port is the Andaman Island capital of Port Blair. I think most of you will do the tour with the spice farm, rubber plantation, and island tour, so that's the one I will be on. Aaron and Hilary, I think this is the most likely place for you to find your pigeon." The couple exchanged an excited glance. Hannah continued, "For everyone else, there are plenty of other tour options. You might want to capture the colours of the markets and the downtown, for example. You can even choose to travel up the river by kayak, if you want to get shots from the water.

"We have one more day at sea before an early arrival into Port Blair in South Andaman. You have plenty of time tomorrow to set up your equipment and ask me anything you like. I will be available for whatever questions you might want answered and to help you with cameras tomorrow. Feel free to drop by after breakfast. We have secured this room for the whole morning tomorrow, just for us.

"After that, we have one sea day between Port Blair and Yangon (that's the new name for Rangoon, for those who don't know). That gives you the opportunity to vet your photos from Andaman Island and check your settings are working for you before we get to Myanmar.

"Please consider your optional outings for Myanmar. Buses with baggage handlers will collect us from the ship on arrival into port, so please make sure you have your camera gear and your overnight bags with you and ready to go. It's a ninety-minute drive into Yangon, so meeting time is 6:00 p.m. sharp in the lobby. Staff can help you ashore with your camera bags if needed.

"We are all going to the People's Park on the first night for the gala evening experience. You are in for a treat! There will be local cuisine, drinks, and desserts, as well as some wonderful and colourful local costumes, and a stage performance. I'm told the park itself is a wonder with fountains, a lake, and a direct view up to the Shwedagon Pagoda.

"We have chosen a central hotel for our two-night stay ashore. I will still be easily accessible for any questions or problems during our visit to Yangon."

Hannah paused for breath and took a sip of tea before continuing. "Our first full day in Yangon is our joint excursion. This is an orientation tour of downtown Yangon as well as a visit to the Royal Barge on Kan Daw Gyi Lake. The highlight of course is a visit to the Shwedagon Pagoda, so make sure you have plenty of memory sticks for your cameras. Oh, and spare batteries, but I don't need to tell you that, right?

"Our second night, after dinner, is our get-together on the rooftop of the Summit Parkview for some amazing night photos, using our drones. Should be a lot of fun, and we'll even throw in a late supper and drinks, but not too many lest you can't drive—your drones, that is." Hannah chuckled. "That will kick off at ten o'clock—past your bedtime, Simon; I'm sorry." She smiled at her husband, knowing how bored he got with all of this.

"Then my suggestion is Bago, the ancient Mon capital, for our last day. On the way there, we stop at the World War II cemetery for those who had relatives working on the Burma Railway; then there are more stupas and reclining Buddhas in Old Bago. As usual, you have other choices if that tour does not appeal.

"After that, it's a pretty full schedule of Ports as we visit Phuket in Thailand — no, Jock, I did pronounce it correctly — then onto Malaysia for Langkawi, Penang, and Kuala Lumpur, before heading into Singapore for two days.

"Well, that's it from me for now. Enjoy your afternoon tea. I will be here for as long as you need me for questions and answers. Come back in the morning with your cameras if you have specific setting-related issues. Enjoy!"

Jock approached her, as the others started to natter in the background. "How did you get permission for the drones Hannah?"

"Oh Jock" she cringed "What a nightmare.

"For each country I had to show that we had a contract for professional photos for travel brochures or magazines for our different home countries, which I managed to arrange with your help, thankfully. Then I had to fill out a zillion forms and attach copies of the purchase documents for each drone. Thankfully every one of you still had those and emailed them to me." Hannah continued "Then I had to approach the Ministry for Tourism in each country to seek their approval for a temporary import. It was horrendous."

"Good Heavens" Jock snickered "Glad it was you and not us."

"Honestly, then I had to repeat it all for every single drone" Hannah remembered with anger " If I had not been able to download the forms, and then just change names and serial numbers, I think I would have given up"

"Guess there's a lesson there for next time" Jock said

"There may not be a next time, if we have to take drones" Hannah stated emphatically.

"And then to add insult to injury, the customs people in Chennai didn't even ask for the import permits when we arrived at the airport" Hannah shook her head "which is probably just as well or we would have missed the ship"

"Yes but you forget we had come through the airport about six hours ahead of you." Jock reminded her. "So they had been looking at paper permits for drones all day as we each arrived."

"Of course" Hannah reflected "I should have thought of that"

"But the ship needed the paperwork anyway" Jock added

"Oh, of course. They had to have copies of everything for their Port Agents for each country. Maybe that's why we didn't have too many problems dockside in Chennai" Hannah tried to control her frustration." Seriously though, all that paperwork; talk about killing trees!"

4

PORT BLAIR

"Welcome to Port Blair. A tropical thirty-three degrees Celsius, or ninety-eight degrees Fahrenheit, with high humidity in the forecast for today in the Andaman Islands," announced the cruise director. "Please remember your hats, sunscreen, and water bottles when going ashore. Enjoy your day."

Hannah explained to her group that thanks to the British claiming it for yet another penal colony, the Andaman Islands had remained a part of India since the days of the old Commonwealth. A tropical paradise closer to the Burmese coast than to the coast of India, Port Blair was a strategic naval and trading location in the Indian Ocean. It was a busy township with a hundred thousand residents, and it was quickly apparent that the Andamese were well-off compared to most regions of India. Lush tropical gardens, fat cows and goats, plenty of water — a real paradise. There was no commerce to speak of, mostly subsistence farmers, with only rubber production being sent to the mainland to earn income. But the Andamese paid no taxes, had free medical care, and even free schooling including university if they wanted to study on the mainland. People seemed happy. There was no crime because there was no escaping the island unless you wanted to spend two days at sea.

Nathan, a member of the U.K. Coast Guard, had an affinity with all things relating to the sea, so he and Amanda had chosen the morning Museum tours. They would be taken to Samudrika Museum to see the local marine exhibits, then onto the Anthropological Museum and finish with a visit to Aberdeen Markets.

Philip Ngu, an accountant from Singapore, had opted to spend the day exploring the township on his own. He had expressed a desire to get to know the locals, and the steamy tropical climate would not worry him, it was very similar to temperatures back home. Hannah knew he would wander around photographing daily life in downtown Port Blair.

Hannah and the remainder of her group boarded the bus for the day tour. Inexplicably, the bus was fitted with an air conditioner that did not work. The tour guide said the air conditioning would come on when the bus started moving. Sadly, what he meant was the wind would blow through the open windows. Simon looked at his wife and raised an unimpressed eyebrow.

They drove in through the township, first stopping at Aberdeen Bazaar, the centre of the universe for the locals. A central clock tower was the town's main landmark. The market was not only the spot to shop for fruits and vegetables, fish and meat, but also where day tours and accommodation could be arranged.

The colours, sights, and smells of the bazaar were strangely welcoming as they watched the locals going about their day. Cameras whirred and photos were captured as women in colourful saris walked past the group. Throughout the bazaar they were surrounded by handwoven baskets piled high with fruit and carried on heads, horns honking, cows reclining, and snarled traffic — but all somehow friendly. The group spent time walking through the market, inhaling the scent of fresh spices grown locally. Some bought wood carvings, while others grabbed cool drinks at stalls.

Their tour guide related the history of the Cellular Jail, one of the island's most renowned sites. "Vast numbers of political prisoners from the Indian Rebellion of 1857 prompted the need for a new jail. The building was constructed as several wings of large isolation cells. Prisoners were subjected to solitary confinement with regular whippings, and suffered hard labour in cruel conditions. They either died of starvation, disease, or hanging. After it finally closed, the jail was transformed into a national monument to their freedom fighters. Only three wings remain of the original six."

Port Blair was mostly steep hills, so the bus had to climb out of town. They stopped for a quick photo opportunity just past the airport, at pastoral flatlands alongside a waterway, with palms and birds alone in the environment. They wondered what they were supposed to be looking at in this area so devoid of activity.

"This is the lake made by the tsunami of December 2006," the tour guide said. "The same waves that hit Banda Aceh also roared north into the Andamans. The wave came gushing inland, up the creek. It pushed away houses and people, leaving many dead and dozens of homes destroyed. There was so much water arriving into that large paddock beneath the airport that the lake is still there nearly a decade later."

A hush fell over the Club members. They captured their images on camera — and in heads and hearts — before returning to the bus.

Onward the road wound up and down hills and valleys toward a spice farm, a government-run agriculture station. Here they learned that locals were taught farming methods and how to care for spice trees and home-grown botanicals. The group was shown black pepper, cinnamon, bay leaf, nutmeg, and cloves growing at the teaching farm, as well as dozens of other varieties of spices and ornamental plants, plus a whole section given over to medicinal plants.

The tour guide pointed out that the gardens also carried an amazing array of flowers — an abundance of orchids grew in the tropical heat and rain of the

Andamans. The colours inspired a flurry of activity among the Camera Club.

Oh the colours, Hannah had been delighted. Her camera whirred as the images were captured.

They returned to the bus an hour later, covered in sweat from the heat of the day. Simon was now grateful for the "air conditioning" when the bus started up. The shade of the rainforest brought quick relief, and the heat was soon forgotten as they traversed the island toward the next stop.

A regional high school had extended an invitation to see the facilities given to local education. The principal's office was large, with an electric fan grinding in the corner. The monthly exams were in progress, so the classrooms were hushed, but heads peeked up, curious about their foreign guests. Teenagers were making models in one room; Bunsen burners were being used in another.

The last room in the block proved the most interesting.

"Come quickly" Laura had grabbed Hannah's arm and propelled her toward the end class room. Girls were learning a folk song and dance and were happy to perform for their guests. Everyone cheered their thanks and appreciation for the demonstration.

"Weren't they great?" Laura had smiled at Hannah

"Wonderful," she had replied "just wonderful."

The tour guide led them out into the small side garden, where the pupils had their own herb garden.

Here they would tend their plots and learn how to fix what ailed them, a lost art in a civilised world. Fond farewells were waved out classroom windows. The tourists left with smiles on their faces.

Farther up into the highlands, the road narrowed and turned to gravel. The villages were smaller and there were fewer people to be seen. Local women, babes on hips, were walking into town to collect their daily needs. Old folk sat on chairs on front decks. *Some things are the same all over the world,* Hannah mused.

The bus rocked along a narrow road through the rainforest until it came to a stop opposite a gate. Everyone bundled out, realizing they had arrived at the rubber plantation.

The plantation manager introduced himself as Jayant and explained their farming methods. "We have about three thousand rubber trees here on about twenty acres. All of our trees are tended by hand each day. They are the island's only source of export income. Rubber trees grow to nearly forty metres in tropical environments, needing lots of rain and lots of hot days. The trees need to mature for six years before they produce the milky-white latex sap. Only then can the 'tappers' include them in their rounds. They gently shave a thin layer off the tree bark using a curved knife like this," he explained, showing them his cutting implement and beginning to carve into a tree.

"The depth of the cut is important. If it is too deep it will only wound the tree, too shallow and the milk will not ooze. Making a spiral cut around the tree allows the latex to flow freely like blood from a small wound. The latex seeps down the length of the cut and into a collection pot, just here." He pointed to the cup that was partly full. "The tree will only bleed for a couple of hours, so we start early in the day. That way, collection is complete before the sun can start drying the latex in the cup. As you can see, the liquid looks and feels like a cross between milk and household glue."

"How much do you get from each tree?" asked Gordon.

"A couple of litres. Then we have to rest the tree for a day before we tap it again. Trees are tapped for about twenty-five years before they are brought down and the area replanted with new saplings."

Jayant led them back to the work sheds where the liquid was being treated with a preservative to stop coagulation. The milk would then be heated before being pressed into small sheets of rubber, ready for export. The sheets were dried on racks around the grounds.

"The process hasn't changed much in hundreds of years," Jayant explained. "Originally, the latex was collected and made into balls. Some of the early producers would dip their feet into the latex liquid, allow it to dry, and then dip and dry again and again, until they could peel a 'shoe' from their feet. Then 'shoes' were smoked over hot embers until the rubber hardened. Later they realized they could coat their clothes in the liquid, and this was the first waterproofing that we know of. These days, rubber is used mostly for tyres and not much else."

The latex smelled bad to begin with, and the smells associated with the process were worse, so the group walked quickly through the workshop and on into the plantation beyond.

"Oh my, look at that bird," shouted Hilary. Aaron slammed the camera in her direction and started clicking wildly. Whatever the bird was, it appeared to be a ground dweller, so it was slow enough for Aaron to chase down. He photographed it in its natural setting as it returned to its nest. He declared it to have been a double-banded sand grouse, but his wife disagreed.

The group returned to the bus and it pulled away onto the dusty road, passing a group of local women walking into town. Within fifteen minutes, they were back on the coastal road.

The guide told them they were coming up on a lovely place to photograph, with resorts and deck chairs on a sandy beach. Honeymoon heaven for Indian nationals, apparently, and a very pretty spot. Most of the passengers made a dash for the water to wade for a few minutes, cooling their feet. They made the most of the chance to take photos along the beach lined with palm trees, unaware of danger lurking close by in the form of crocodiles.

They noticed old Japanese outposts built into the side of the cliffs, a reminder of the islands occupation during the Second World War. As they left the beach-front, the bus passed holiday resorts and modern ho-tels along an inviting shoreline. There seemed to be plenty of opportunities for kayaking and scuba diving, if they were ever back this way again.

Coming back into the township of Port Blair, they saw large sports fields, swimming pools, and ten-nis courts. This area seemed more modern than the Aberdeen Bazaar they had visited in the morning. They waved as they drove past Philip Ngu, who was walking back toward the port.

An exhausted group returned to the ship, weary from their day out. Nathan and Amanda had beaten them back by two hours and were swanning around the pool deck. But an hour later, the others were all show-ered and refreshed, ready to meet for drinks before din-ner. Every member of the group was quickly caught up with sharing images captured throughout the day, ex-cept Hannah's husband and Nathan's bride — but the beers were cold, there was a nice sauvignon blanc for Amanda, the hors d'oeuvres had been served and the lounge was air-conditioned. Laughter permeated the air.

5

MYANMAR COAST

The sun rose earlier than Hannah the next day. With about a hundred kilometres before the Burmese coast, most of the day was to be spent at sea.

Simon pushed for their daily walk around the deck after a very late breakfast. As they emerged from the interior of the ship, they could see crowds of passengers lining the handrail around the promenade deck. All were peering out to sea.

"What's going on?" Hannah queried.

"Oh, Look" Simon's tall frame peered over the other heads "a fishing fleet."

Fishing boats floated in the Andaman Sea all around the Quest. They appeared to be about the size of large canoes, arranged in lines, with fishing nets strung between them. Here, in the middle of the ocean, these small boats would anchor for weeks on end. Supply ships visited them regularly to collect their catch and deliver anything they might need.

"Good Lord, they're everywhere." Hannah had been overwhelmed with the unexpected sight on the water around them.

There were hundreds of these lines of boats speckled around them across the ocean on either side. Each line consisted of five or six boats. What a photo opportunity! Hannah had found a gap against the railing and slid into it.

Hannah was enthralled by the boats and their apparently lazy idleness as they bobbed in the ocean, anchored in place. The colours were muted in the sunlight. The solemnity of these sentinels of the sea, and the sheer numbers of them, were mind boggling. Her camera whirred.

Simon interrupted her "That's odd" he said

"What is, love?" Hannah barely looked his way, continuing to shoot frame after frame.

"The water looks dirty, like we are churning up the bottom" Simon responded. "How can that be, we're in the middle of the ocean?"

Hannah looked over the side of the ship. The water was muddy beneath them. "Well the fleet appears to be anchored so it can't be that deep, can it?"

Then the midday announcement came over the loudspeakers.

"Good afternoon. This is the captain with today's noon report. We are at the lowest draft of any voyage, with only ten metres of water beneath us in this part of the ocean. The draft of the vessel is six metres, so we are slowed to just ten knots in this channel."

"That explains it," Simon declared. "It's a bit different from sailing from Guam last year over the Mariana Trench. What was that — ten kilometres deep? Eleven?"

"Mmm, something like that," Hannah replied, deep in thought as she focused the next shot. "Isn't this amazing?"

After lunch, a nap was a real luxury. Given that they would be out late this evening, both Hannah and Simon soon succumbed to slumber for an hour. When they surfaced, the vessel had just entered the Yangon River, and life in Myanmar was coming into view.

The couple had emerged from their cabin and were walking to the elevators to take them up to the top deck. As they passed a window, they could see wonderful little villages lining the river banks. Cottages constructed of palm fronds dotted the landscape. Fishing boats crowded the water. Children played on the shore. There were no roads to be seen this far down river.

Hannah noticed a glint on the horizon, and another in a nearby field.

"Is that a stupa?" she asked her husband. "Can you see?"

Simon drew out the binoculars. "Sure is," he said, "just a little one on the hill and another in that field."

"Good Lord!" Hannah said. "I didn't expect them to be on every farm. I thought that was only in Bagan, in the north. Gotta get this." She dashed outside and swung her camera upward and was lost to her photography yet again.

Simon had strolled the length of the promenade deck while his wife was lost to her passion. *She might be ready by the time I finish a lap around the deck,* he thought.

As he rounded the corner at the stern, he saw Jock and Gordon ahead of him. They were deep in conversation. It seemed intense, so Simon was hesitant to approach them. They looked like they were arguing.

"It's not right" said Gordon "and I don't feel comfortable with it"

"Well you should have thought about that before we agreed to come" Jock had snarled back at him. "You knew we had money problems, so don't complain about it now!"

"Afternoon, Gents." Simon pretended not to have overheard their remarks. "Looking forward to tonight?"

"Yes, of course" Gordon had smiled in an off-handed way.

Simon kept walking, but wondered what the argument was about. *Lovers tiff I guess,* he thought, *we all have them.*

Two hours later the pier came into view, with the landmark twin cranes marking the location of the industrial port. The *Quest* slid gently into dock at Myanmar Maritime Terminals (known as MTT) at

Thilawa, downriver from Yangon. Anchors were released and mooring ropes tied off.

A multitude of genuinely air-conditioned buses lined the wharf, ready to load passengers for tonight's festivities.

Hannah's heart raced, her breath quickened. But she knew she needed to keep her excitement to herself.

Welcome to Myanmar.

6

YANGON

MTT Port was huge. The dock area was long enough to hold eight vessels the size of the *Quest*. The variety of infrastructure, personnel, and equipment seemed to scream "industrial port."

The draft of the ship would not allow the vessel to sail up the Yangon River into the small port in Yangon proper. But at this point, the river was wide; the vessel had easily swung around and slid into the dock.

In front of the *Quest*, a large car carrier disgorged its contents. This process continued for over twenty-four hours before the ship would finally be ready to leave. Hannah noticed several carparks large enough to hold hundreds of imported cars. This surprised her; it was not what she expected to see in an ancient land.

On the outskirts of the fenced port area, warehouses and office blocks covered the needs of cold storage and workers alike. Armed guards supplied security at the port gates, slowing vehicles for inspection and checking documents before allowing access.

The waterfront was strewn with thousands of lengths of timber, stacked ready for loading onto cargo ships. Trees were the one thing Myanmar still had plenty of.

"Guess I needn't have worried about killing trees" Hannah had commented as they saw the timber stacks. "They clearly have plenty of them."

"Well this certainly is the middle of nowhere isn't it?" Laura Glenn stood alongside Hannah on the promenade deck. "You can't even see a town from here."

"They said it was ninety minutes to get into town, so I guess we are in the middle of nowhere" Hannah replied.

Hannah really liked Laura. She was a few years older than Hannah but was full of vitality. Laura had a zest for life that was contagious. She was also one of the most personable women Hannah had ever known. Nobody had guessed that Laura was sixty seven years old, even her hair was still naturally coloured, not greying like Hannah's.

"I'm surprised at the Port facilities though" Laura noted "Who would have thought they would have such a modern port?"

"It looks so organised" Hannah had been happy to continue the conversation. "Just as well, if they are going to get us all into town in time for tonight's celebrations at the People's Park"

"How many are going?" Laura asked

"About five hundred, I think. That would explain all the buses on the dock." Hannah continued. "There's a lot of activity down there"

The two women peered over the side of the ship. Beneath them the dock was teeming with activity. The ship's crew were loading pallets of melons onto the vessel. Ship's porters pushed catering trolleys across to a bus at the head of the line. The *Quest's* photographers were setting up dockside, ready to take the inevitable port photos of passengers arriving in a new destination. The Cruise Director stood at the bottom of the gangway directing his staff toward numbered vehicles. He had to ensure all vehicles were ready to accept passengers when clearance was given. It would be another twenty minutes before they were given permission to start disembarkation.

It was hot and humid, as the first passengers clambered down the gangway onto the concrete dock. They hurried across to their designated buses. Hannah's group had been assigned a vehicle of their own to accommodate the additional cases full of photography equipment and overnight bags. They will be one of only a few groups staying overnight in Yangon.

The group was boisterous and surprisingly loud as they manhandled their gear toward waiting luggage trolleys.

"Careful with that." Ted growled at the porter who fumbled the drone case onto the luggage trolley.

"Will you please take my camera bag?" little Sophie Galena politely asked the next porter, as she struggled with her drone case and her overnight bag. All of her gear was collected and added to the second trolley, ready to be sent to the bus. The lonely little Italian spinster from Bari worked as a shipping clerk, so she understood how the docks worked better than most of the group.

"Mind the way you load that drone case." Gordon complained as his luggage was added to the growing pile.

Simon carried their overnight bag on his shoulder as he strolled across to the bus assigned to take them into Yangon. He was happy to be out of the jostling surrounding the gear being loaded. *You'd think they were carrying gold not bloody drones* he thought as he walked past them.

Hannah had smiled at him knowingly, and shook her head. She understood Simon was frustrated by the importance given to the camera gear. He was just here for a holiday.

Hannah had to wait until all the gear was loaded. She thanked the three porters who had packed the gear for them. She gave them the okay to push the heavy trolleys to the waiting vehicle where the gear would be transferred onto the bus.

Once everyone was seated on the bus, the tour guide introduced himself as the bus pulled away from the pier. This slight man, wizened and grey, looked like a breath of wind would blow him over. His voice, though, was soft and clearly educated, with a lilt reminiscent of an English accent.

"Good afternoon. Welcome to Myanmar. I am U Win, your guide for the next few days." Jock, seated behind Hannah, gently tugged a lock of her hair to let her know what he thought of the guide's name. U Win did not seem to notice and continued. "Life is about choices, and you have made the choice to come to Myanmar. We are very thankful you have made that choice. Tourism is important to our economy and is a growing industry that is given priority support by the government.

"I will be giving you a little history as background to the places we will be visiting. I hope this will help you to understand the development of Myanmar, the culture, and the people of this land.

"Our homeland is often referred to as the Land of the Pagoda. There is no mountain, no village, no place without a pagoda. You will see them in every direction. The most famous and most important to our people is the Shwedagon. It houses several relics of Buddha, and is said to have been erected twenty-five hundred years ago. The dome is covered with gold, and semiprecious stones adorn the crown. It is truly a sight to behold. It is revered by us as a place of meditation and worship. You will be asked to dress reverently when visiting the pagoda tomorrow.

"You will see monks in prayer and locals in meditation. Please keep your voices lowered and respectful at all times around the pagoda complex. Please do not remove anything, no matter how small a trinket. It will be missed. Our religion deems this to bring bad karma to you. Instead there will be stalls where you can purchase souvenirs and gifts. One should use those options, as it is never OK to remove any part of the pagoda or its decorations.

"There are only a few areas where women are not allowed. One is the upper eastern platform of the Shwedagon Pagoda. This is the site of a Buddha statue believed to grant wishes, so it is off-limits to women." There was a rustle of discontent from some of the women in the group. U Win smiled gently and went on. "In the Eastern Prayer Hall, there is a wishing Buddha for women. You will know him by his upturned palms, suggesting he has something to give away.

"No woman should ever touch a monk, nor hand him anything. Monks are also not allowed to touch women, nor take anything from their hands. When giving alms to monks, place them in his offering bowl, don't give them to him directly.

"In Myanmar, when you want to take someone's photo, you should always respectfully ask the person's permission.

"Folklore and religion are central to our daily life. We have strong beliefs about how to conduct ourselves and how to respect our religion. Like most sons, I, too, served for a while as a monk when I was a child. Families believe it is an honour to serve and will bring their sons to be inducted, usually between three and twelve years of age.

"For over twenty-five years, I have been guiding tours, so I understand you will have many questions along the way. Please ask me anything. I also teach English at a high school in Yangon, so I hope you will have no trouble understanding me." U Win smiled his beatific smile again.

"Our drive into Yangon this afternoon will take about ninety minutes. It is not such a long way, about twenty kilometres, but the roads are not as good as you might be used to in your country. The roads have to service all communities, so progress can be slow. You will see many motorbikes as we travel through the local villages. These have become very popular in the last few years. They were not allowed prior to the year 2000.

"Myanmar loves festivals, and tonight we take great pride in welcoming you to join us in this ancient tradition. We are headed for the People's Park, where you will be welcomed by magical images, cultural shows, elephant dances, local food, and traditional handmade goods. I hope you will enjoy the evening."

Outside the port gates, there were little stalls selling food and drinks. Taxis and hire cars waited for solo travellers who wanted to explore on their own. Tonight, though, only a few stayed behind.

Along the roadside, over the next few kilometres, workers were toiling in the fields and road crews were repairing the road surface. The convoy of buses had a police escort to ensure progress was as swift as possible.

While it was nice to be treated like VIPs, Hannah was slightly uncomfortable with this. "I wouldn't want the locals to think we see ourselves as more important than they are. I think it sends the wrong message, don't you, Si?"

"Yes, quite possibly. Makes me wonder how much longer it would take without the police outriders, though," he replied.

The rolling fields were dotted with cottages, mostly made from wall panels of woven grass with bamboo supports. There was water in the fields and crops seemed abundant. The roadside stalls carried what must have been thousands upon thousands of watermelons. Each farmlet had its own stall, and no one in their group had ever seen so many melons. They were stacked over a metre high for almost five kilometres.

Each vista held at least one stupa. Hannah noticed that their sizes varied from as small as a fountain to as large as a village church. *And that's what they are*, she thought. Some were simple red-earth structures, while others were gilded with gold leaf. Their coatings danced reflections as the afternoon sun hit the exteriors. Others were simply whitewashed and sat elegantly against the backdrop of village life. It was immediately apparent how much these stupas were a part of everyday life for the people of Myanmar, just as Catholic churches were to Italians.

Villagers were still active as the evening closed in. Food stalls were abundant, with restaurants set up with little plastic tables and chairs in an array of colours. Other stalls were selling cloth or home supplies and groceries. As they approached the first village, they were delighted with their first introduction to a gilded stupa. It stood about ten metres high. The roar of camera shutters was almost deafening on the bus, as it followed the winding road toward Yangon.

Within an hour, the bus had reached the outskirts of the city. The single lane road opened into a three-lane thoroughfare in each direction. Little vehicles, trucks, motorbikes, and plenty of bicycles vied for space. Simon pointed out the handful of traffic lights, only at major intersections.

The fields had rolled into a suburban landscape of apartment buildings, retail outlets, business offices, medical centres and the like. No one had really expected to see a modern city, yet that was what they had found. Yangon was a modern city with beautifully green parks and abundant trees along the suburban roadside as they arrived on the city fringes. They had been told that the river at this point was more than a kilometre and a half wide. They crossed a long bridge to enter the city proper, but were still eight kilometres from downtown.

Another bridge over a smaller tributary and several traffic roundabouts later, the convoy rolled past the Kandawgyi Lake, a replica Royal Barge dominating the scene. The afternoon light was fading, but they could make out the size and colours of the barge. The photographers snapped away, capturing frame after frame on cameras of all different types until the barge had disappeared from sight. When some rumbling about having missed an important landmark began to emerge from the passengers, U Win reassured them that they would have a dedicated stop at the Royal Barge during the next day's itinerary.

As the bus pushed closer to downtown, the expectation on board began to build. By the time they got their first glimpse of a golden glow on the top of Singuttara Hill, the excitement was palpable.

The bus approached the southern entrance to Shwedagon, the structure towering over the city. The evening lights were now aglow. The night sky was suddenly filled with the enormous golden pagoda. Shwedagon flashed past them in a microsecond. The "oohs" and "ahs" around the vehicle echoed almost in unison.

It vanished from sight as quickly as it appeared, teasing them mercilessly as they scurried farther into the night.

"Oh my God!" Hannah nudged Simon so hard his upper arm would show a bruise tomorrow. "Did you see that?"

"Good Lord, that is absolutely stunning," Simon replied, rubbing his shoulder.

The sentiment was echoed around the bus, with partners prodding each other in case they had missed the glimpse of gold above them. Few had been able to catch this first peek on digital "film," so quickly had it come and gone.

They were now less than a kilometre from the People's Park, and the convoy of buses started to slow. The procession turned off Ahlone Road in Dagon Township.

In single file the buses entered a large grassy parking area. Doors opened almost simultaneously, delivering guests in a flurry of feet hitting the ground as they stepped down from each vehicle.

It was dark now, and hard to see in which direction the crowds were headed. A faint glow of candlelight became apparent about fifty metres ahead of them, at the edge of the parking lot.

The wide path, lit only by candles, looked like it led to some kind of fairyland. The visitors strolled beneath an avenue of trees. A hush fell over the crowd as they stepped carefully in the darkness. Anticipation grew with the approach to the park entrance. The crowd ambled forward toward the avenue ahead, stretching left and right as it emerged beyond the canopy of trees.

Suddenly the area ahead was filled with water. In the air all around them, the spray from an array of massive fountains was lit by a revolving rainbow of colours. Spouting six metres into the air, the spray of the first fountain was aflame with orange hues, vivid against the black of the night sky. A silhouette of human shapes appeared in front of the fountain as each person stopped to take their photos and soak up the ambience of such a wonderful sight.

Beyond that spectacle, another monument with water sprays encircling it was lit in vivid lime green with blue and orange spotlights. Stone elephants adorned it in layers around its centre, while spotlights surged toward the stars above.

The Parliament Building was lit at the far end of the avenue, but no one was looking that way. All eyes were drawn in the other direction, along the avenue to their right.

Above them, towering over the landscape, was the splendid golden pagoda known as Shwedagon. Magnificent and overpowering all at once, it sat on a terraced hill at the end of the avenue, its golden dome lit with hundreds of spotlights from below. This "wonder of the world" had all the tourists enthralled. The glow emanating from the hill was spellbinding, and few could draw their eyes away.

There they stood, in turn, soaking up the magnificence in front of them. Nothing could have prepared them for this sight. It was truly awesome. The crowd nudged forward for the next in line to look on this wonder. They were each propelled along until they could no longer see the pagoda and someone else was having a turn.

The crowd wandered onward, across a bridge, passing colourful characters dressed in traditional costume along the way. The colours were enchanting, the silver and gold threads on their costumes alluring, speaking of a time long ago when wealth was displayed in dress.

Dancers swayed to traditional songs as ancient instruments worked their spell in the background. Hannah found the atmosphere mesmerizing. Local children joined parents and siblings in a fascinating display of culture in performances all around the grounds.

Cultural bands played while children danced around them. The audience was enthralled with a never ending performance on the central stage. Dancers, colourful "dragons" and playful "pups" dressed in traditional Asian style, entertained the crowds.

Each guest was greeted by the official welcoming party. Hannah had been delighted to meet the Captain of the *Quest* as well as the local Minister for Tourism. She had stopped to have her photograph taken by the ship's photographers. Hannah was slow to move away, but she was drawn into the entrance to the cultural displays where she was presented with a floral necklace and a little wooden crafted ornament, as a memento of the evening.

Hannah would remember this enchanting evening for a long time to come. Local artisans had set up shopping stalls by the gate, where hand-painted paper parasols, local lacquerware, and artwork were for sale. Food stalls beckoned the crowd farther into the park. The local cuisine, based on a mix of Chinese and Indian traditions, scented the air with wonderful aromas. There was a group of people standing around one of the outdoor barbecues, as local chefs turned produce on the hotplate.

Jennifer Zweers was unlikely to refuse any of the local dishes on offer tonight. She loved her food, and was enjoying the variety on offer. At fifty three years of age, this lonely widow was clearly overweight. Everyone had their strengths though and Jennifer had found hers was her creativity. When she wasn't behind a camera lens, she was cooking up a storm for friends or producing beautiful hand crafted quilts. She had found happiness again.

"Oh, have you tried this?" she drooled to a complete stranger standing next to her. Jennifer licked her fingers as she finished the plate of food in her hand.

"What's in it?" her new companion asked.

"This one is the traditional *Mohinga*. It's a rice noodle in fish gravy. And that one" she pointed to the next food stall "is flavoured noodles with chicken in a coconut soup. So delicious!"

"Have you had any of those?" Jock had joined Jennifer, and was pointing to the tray of snacks being offered around.

"No, not yet. What are they?" Jennifer had already moved toward the tray on offer, keen to try more of the local delicacies.

"Well this one is some kind of seaweed jelly with coconut milk on top. Sounds weird but tastes great." Jock explained. "And this one is a rice dumpling filled with coconut, and it's surprisingly good." Jock knew it would not take much convincing for Jennifer to sample the *mont lone gyi*.

Hannah and Simon couldn't choose between the savoury lentil pancakes and the crispy finger foods with plenty of spice, so they ate them both, and followed them up with an overly sweet yet delicious dessert, the humble *jiggery*, made with glutinous rice, milk, sugar, and coconut.

"Do they have something that isn't too spicy?" asked timid Sophie Galena. Hannah helped her to choose several dishes to try.

The group was relishing the local cuisine, which included a variety of snacks, main dishes, and sweets. They agreed that the most popular dish of the night was the *bein mont*, a type of rice pancake.

Tonight they had learned a lot about the food of Myanmar. The rice was plentiful but beef was rare. Fresh chicken, duck, pork, mutton, and fish seasoned with onion, garlic, turmeric, tamarind juice, dried prawns, fish sauce, chili, and ginger were simmered and served with a relish of preserves. Desserts were rarely served unless guests were being entertained.

This was the largest group the festival had ever attracted. Cruise staff wandered among guests offering cold beers, ciders, and wine that had been brought over from the *Quest*, enjoying the excuse to attend the event themselves.

There was so much to absorb that the cameras never stopped. Some guests were still hungry because they had skipped the opportunity to eat, in order to capture the scene on camera. Nobody minded, this was a once in a lifetime opportunity and had to be absorbed to be remembered. It was carnival-like and joyous.

The evening drew to a close all too soon. The crowd was eventually persuaded to reboard the buses for the journey back to the ship. For Hannah's Camera Club, the journey to their night's accommodation was so short they could easily have walked it.

Their bus pulled away from the back of the People's Park, slid past the Parliament buildings, turned left again onto Ahlone Road, and pulled to the right into the entrance of the Summit Parkview hotel.

Chosen for its central location in the heart of Yangon, this quaint Myanmar hotel had traditional architecture with pleasant manicured gardens. It sat facing the verdant People's Park. This area of town was home to embassies, museums, and shopping centres. It would only be a ten-minute walk to Shwedagon and a five-minute drive to get downtown.

The hotel's other defining feature was the view from the bedrooms straight across the skyline to the

Shwedagon Pagoda. Hannah found the view magnificent in its evening coat of light, and was sure it would be just as inspiring in the light of day.

She had selected this hotel over other candidates for the rooftop viewing point. The group would be able to set up an evening camera shoot, undisturbed by other hotel guests.

The lobby was unpretentious and reasonably spacious. There was an outdoor courtyard that led onto the inviting pool deck. Hotel staff greeted the group, provided keys, and sent the luggage up to the rooms.

Hannah briefly called them together. "Folks, breakfast starts at six thirty in the morning just there in the café. Please be on time, so we can leave at eight o'clock sharp. U Win wants to get us out before the heat of the day. Sleep well, and we shall see you in the morning. Good night!"

"Don't let the bed bugs…" Gordon started to sing

"Oh shut up you old fool" Jock poked him in the ribs.

7

DOWNTOWN

At precisely 8:02 a.m., U Win ordered the driver to pull out into the morning traffic. They were heading for the centre of town. At Mahabandoola Park, in the heart of Yangon, the group alighted for a photo opportunity at the Sule Pagoda, a landmark from the Mon dynasty.

Nearby were the City Hall, a grand stucco structure, and the National Independence Monument.

While their cameras clicked away, the local vendors descended upon them to sell postcards and trinkets with little success. When you have a good camera, why would you want to buy a postcard?

U Win encouraged them to return in the evening to walk around the city centre, and visit the fruit market and Chinatown for an insight into local life.

The bus moved on through Bogyoke Aung San Market, which had recently been renamed in honour of their national hero. It had previously been known as Scott Market, but whatever the name, the market had been in that same spot for ninety years. If they returned, they would have a chance to visit more than sixteen hundred stalls, selling everything from gemstones and jewellery to fashion, luxury items, and consumer goods.

They pushed farther on to the National Museum, where an early private admission had been arranged. Here they saw the Lion Throne of the last Myanmar king—the only one remaining of the original nine, which had been carved simultaneously on a single day in AD 1220. There was also royal regalia from the nineteenth century and other priceless artefacts. Photos were not allowed here, so the visit was relatively short.

They resumed the journey around Yangon past the rail yards and the old port on the Yangon River, which was still in use in the centre of town. The bus wound its way around the growing city that had come to life for its working day.

It was a thankful group that arrived at the lake with its gardens and public spaces, including the Karaweik Royal Barge, which they had been whisked past last night. It was a popular photo spot that told a tale of days gone by, although the barge itself was only a reproduction. With its dragon head leading the vessel, it had a small palace-style structure on its deck. Resplendent in gold edging and gorgeous royal-green and crimson paint, the replica vessel was permanently docked and was a popular wedding venue.

The lakeside park was a pleasant spot with refreshment stands and restaurants. Plenty of shade trees offered welcome relief from the growing heat. The group took an early lunch at the food stalls along the lake before re-joining the bus.

"What a lovely spot." Laura was heard to say.

Heading back into town, they made a stop at the giant reclining Buddha at Chaukhtatgyi Pagoda. Having respectfully removed their shoes and socks and covered any bare legs or arms, they entered the inner zone. Housed in a simple metal-roofed shed, the Buddha was immense — nearly fifty metres long, its head some eight metres above the ground. Simon was amused by the whorls of toe prints that were etched under the feet.

A short ride brought them back to the eastern entrance to the great golden stupa known as Shwedagon. Stepping down from the bus, the club members checked that they had their camera gear strung around their necks, backup cameras over their shoulders, and spare batteries and memory sticks in backpacks.

"Are you alright Sophie?" Digby Tennyson checked in case she needed help with her gear.

"Yes thank you" Sophie replied, her little voice barely audible.

Amanda Donaldson watched them load their gear. She was glad she could just enjoy the moment without having to worry about cameras and tripods. She was immensely proud of Nathan's camera work and loved looking through his photos, but she had no interest whatsoever in taking photos herself.

Hannah realised that they had come in through the parking lot so she had missed seeing the pair of massive *chinthe* (stone lions) at the entrance to the walkway, and the bas reliefs of chariots and royal processions on its walls. *Never mind - you can't have everything* she thought.

They climbed the few steps to the entrance booth, paid for admission, removed shoes and socks, and placed them on a rack.

"I hope they're still there when we get back" Digby had joked.

Attendants at the stupa checked their clothing for suitability before granting them admittance to the religious site.

Flower stalls brought the heady scent of fresh blossoms. They provided the strands of flowers locals bought as offerings to drape around the Buddha statues and planetary sites when they reached the temple floor on the terraced hill above.

"The flowers are beautiful" Maggie Hooper whispered to her neighbour. Maggie loved the ancient lifestyles and customs. She was known for her alternative attitudes and her op shop clothing. Maggie was a gay rights activist in her trendy home town of Paddington in Sydney. Everything about her showed she was an art teacher.

Fortune-tellers were on hand to tell visitors their karmic future and planetary post (determined by the day of the week on which a person is born). There were currency-exchange booths and stalls selling incense sticks, ceremonial umbrellas, and images of the Buddha. Upstairs there was even an ATM, making it easier for visitors and locals alike to be generous with their offerings.

They were pleased to discover the option to take the elevator up the equivalent of three floors rather than have to ascend the 118 steps in the covered walkway.

So began some of the most memorable hours of their lives.

8

SHWEDAGON

U Win begins his commentary, "Before you visit Shwedagon, it is important that you understand something of the history and significance of this complex. There is a story behind the relics enshrined here at Shwedagon that I want to share briefly with you. It helps to explain the relevance of the pagoda to the people of Myanmar.

"History tells that two brothers, who were merchant traders, came across Buddha resting under a bodhi tree. After they shared some honey cakes with him, he blessed them with eight hairs from his head. These are known as the sacred relics. On their return to Dagon village, later absorbed by a growing Rangoon, the brothers presented the hairs in a ruby casket to the king. The hairs were now sitting in pearls piled to resemble the shape of a stupa.

"When the king opened the casket, it was like stories of opening Pandora's Box. Only this time, instead of releasing evil, the land was blessed with trees suddenly turning to bud and then instantly coming into bloom; miracles were granted, and the blind were given sight. The deaf heard sound for the first time, and the mute found voice — all the usual miracles. But best of all, the sky is said to have rained jewels. Hence, the locals believed the jewels belonged to Buddha.

"Previous relics had been enshrined on Singuttara Hill because it was the highest point of the landscape at fifty-two metres above sea level, so the decision was made to house the relics here. And so the new relics were enshrined on a Full Moon Day, a Wednesday, as it happened." Hannah had read that the days of the week had a deeper meaning for the people of Myanmar than for Westerners.

"A square chamber was built measuring forty-four cubits a side," the guide continued. "Legend has it that the chamber was then filled with layers of jewels, each layer covered with sand and then topped with another layer of gemstones until the chamber was almost full. The final addition was a model ship encrusted with jewels, and on this the relics were placed. The chamber was sealed with a slab of stone covered with gold. They then built a pagoda another forty-four cubits high and gilded it before covering that with six more structures each with a different covering. One was covered in silver, the next in an alloy of copper and gold, then came a bronze covering, then an iron one followed by a marble cover, and then the final brick paya. This became known as Shwe Dagon — the Temple of Dagon Township."

Jock McAdams interjected, "How big is a cubit?"

"Well," U Win replied, "that's not been completely determined because it was essentially the length from the elbow to the tip of the middle finger, and, as we know, people are different sizes, so differing measurements were used. In Egypt, for example, it was commonly about forty-four to forty-five centimetres, but they were also known to use a measurement of about fifty-two centimetres, which later became known as a long cubit. For the sake of the exercise, let's say they used the accepted measure for a common cubit, about forty-five and a half centimetres. That makes the original chamber nearly twenty five square metres, that's 5 metres each side. But remember this was only the inner chamber—a bit like the Egyptians and the king's treasure they buried with the pharaohs, isn't it?

"Of course none of this is proven. It is just folklore, but then I always remember thinking King Arthur and Guinevere were fable characters until I visited their grave sites in Cornwall in the UK."

Jock started to object, "Those Cornwall burial sites are highly speculative. There's no real evidence —" before he felt his partner's sharp elbow in his ribs.

U Win went on with his story, ignoring the interruption. "Exactly when construction of the pagoda began is unknown. Legend has it that Shwedagon has been in existence for some twenty-five hundred years. The first accurate description of it has the size listed at just eight-point-two metres tall, so this would suggest that was the original paya built to house the relics of the first three Buddhas — certainly before the erection of the stupa to house the relics of the fourth Buddha. We expect a new Buddha about every five thousand years, so we are due a new one soon. While start of construction could be exaggerated, documents certainly suggest Shwedagon was visible and well known by the 1039 CE."

"CE?" queried Laura Glenn.

U Win explained, "Yes, CE or Common Era, also known as Anno Domini or AD, which is the Christian way of counting. These both mean the same time period, but local documents all list CE. Anyway, over the years, various kings and queens took to improving Shwedagon, eventually even enlarging the pagoda. Each made it taller and grander than his or her predecessor, until it reached its current height of one hundred metres. Height was added in stages, though. In fact, by the 1300s, it had been built to a height of eighteen metres, and a hundred years later the queen raised it to forty metres; it was she who terraced the hillside. She even paved the terraces, but best of all, she donated her weight in gold to have the structure gilded.

"Her son, not to be outdone, later donated four times his weight in gold to finish the gilding. By the early 1500s, this golden pagoda had become famous. The oldest marked brick that has been found is near the top of the eastern stairway and is inscribed with the year 1485.

"Shwedagon is now considered by the locals to be their most sacred site. Certainly it is their most beautiful. In fact, it is listed as one of the religious wonders of the world!" U Win smiled with satisfaction. "This monument is breathtaking in its intricate architecture and its dazzling views of shining gold and sparkling jewels. You will admire artwork, statues, and even plants, such as flowers and bodhi trees. Rumour has it that there are more riches hidden deep inside the pagoda. It certainly adds to the intrigue, though it has never been proven."

As they stepped from the elevator, the atmosphere was serene but exciting. The group was hushed, the suspense was apparent. They were finally here. On their left they could see a view of the city's modern skyline, with communications towers and high-rises forming a major contrast to their current location. The camera action had started.

On their other side was the roof of the covered walkway. The green corrugated roofing contrasted with the abundant ornate golden-wood carvings that extended the length of each roof panel as it terraced up the hillside. The outlook across the skyline was of trees surrounding the forty-six-hectare complex, growing right up to the boundary of the walkways. Below the lift tower were manicured lawns and landscaped gardens.

They moved out into the sunlight to catch their first glimpse of Shwedagon.

"No way!" Nathan sounded surprised to see this monument up close. "It's enormous!"

"Ha, that's really something." Hilary Swanston was beguiled, her neck craning to see the top of the stupa.

At first, they could only see the spire and none of the complex surrounding it. As they stepped out onto the white-marble-tiled courtyard of the main terrace, they found themselves surrounded by a vast number of pavilions, worship halls, sculptures, and carvings in every direction. The cameras were getting a workout.

"Incredible!" cried Jennifer Zweers, the lonely widow from Hobart in Tasmania.

On the corner they saw a mid-sized temple, white-washed and gleaming against the morning sun, with painted Buddhas hidden in carved niches. Alongside was a prayer hall with black marble flooring that enhanced the serenity of the four large Buddhas sitting in a row within. Dressed in amber silk adorned with red-and-gold embroidery, each Buddha stood a massive four metres tall. Between them were smaller versions in varying sizes. Their china-white faces were beautifully painted with full lips, dark eyes with slender brows under jet-black hair with crowns of gold, and the inevitable elongated ear lobes.

"Oh that's gorgeous!" Everywhere Hannah looked, she found intricate carvings, mostly in gold and wood, but some in plaster whitewash across the roofline leading up to golden spires. Pairs of protective *chinthe* stood guard at the entrance of each temple. Gold lacework inscriptions covered the face of the temple; multiple panels five metres high and three metres wide stood sentinel across the external facade. Gold filigree climbed merrily up the cake layers that made up the decorative roof of the building. The glow of gold was everywhere.

The inner ceiling was painted in royal maroon with gold-painted overlay, depicting the eight planetary posts. Wood carvings adorned the outer ceiling depicting folklore in bas relief. They had not even reached the main courtyard yet, and already they were in awe.

U Win led them around a maze of little alleyways between buildings, until they rounded the corner and entered the main courtyard. With cool marble tiles under their bare feet, they were enthralled to join throngs of people moving clockwise around the structures. The main courtyard was about fifteen metres wide, dappled with shade provided by the buildings and spires around the perimeter of the courtyard. But the main attraction was upward.

Towering above them was Shwedagon, one hundred metres of real gold, spearing straight up into the sky. Necks craned upward as cameras were raised, and shutters began to whir in the mesmerizing golden glow.

"Unbelievable!" declared Laura Glenn.

"Staggering." Gordon replied softly.

"Bloody hell!" erupted from Digby Tennyson, an epithet most unusual for him. Digby was the gentleman of the group, always opening doors or giving up his seat for the ladies. At forty-eight, he was still devilishly handsome but modest enough not to take advantage of it. The single ladies hovered near this Canadian stockbroker wherever he went. Digby was oblivious to them as he recorded GPS locations on their walk around the temple.

U Win was pleased to hear the group appreciate the sight above them. "You are looking at twenty-seven tons of gold leaf plus gold plates made from eight thousand six hundred eighty-eight solid gold bars used on the lower stupa, with another thirteen thousand one hundred fifty-three on the upper part. The top of the stupa is set with more than five thousand diamonds, more than two thousand other gemstones — mostly rubies, emeralds, topaz, and sapphires — and almost fifteen hundred bells, of which four hundred twenty are pure silver; the rest are gold. These are crowned by the orb, whose centrepiece is a single seventy-six-carat diamond that catches and reflects the first and last rays of the sun each day. It has been in place since 1871." The group gasped together at the description of this unique stone.

"You may just be able to discern the vane from ground level. It is also encrusted with jewels and gold, and it alone weighs four hundred nineteen kilos. Above that, the diamond orb carries a total of eighteen hundred carats of diamonds.

"Below the vane is the umbrella shape that we call the *hti*. It is covered with five hundred kilos of gold and more than eighty-three thousand gemstones, and it weighs five tons. It is thirteen metres high and five metres wide."

"Where did all the jewels come from?" asked Hilary Swanston.

"This is an earthquake zone, and because of that seismic activity, the land has always been abundant in gemstones, as most earthquake-prone countries tend to be." U Win was a font of knowledge and clearly enjoyed sharing snippets of information with an admiring crowd.

"Actually," U Win continued, "the pagoda has withstood earthquakes for hundreds of years. In the seventeenth century, it was damaged eight times. Eventually, the quake of 1768 brought down the top of the stupa, which is when it was rebuilt to its current height. They kept the part that came down, and you will see that on the other side of the courtyard as we move around the building. In 1930 there was a massive earthquake that devastated nearby Bago, the ancient Mon capital. Shwedagon only had minor damage from that quake. The following year, though, it suffered a significant fire." U Win was animated in his storytelling.

"We had another quake in the seventies that meant more renovations were required. The entire structure was covered in bamboo scaffolding for repairs to be made. It was Cyclone Nargis in 2008 that has caused the most damage in recent times. Now the whole structure is inspected every five years and regilded or replated as necessary."

"You're kidding," said Maggie Hooper, the middle-aged art teacher. "There is more gold here than at the Catherine Palace in St. Petersburg. Who pays for it?"

"All donated by the locals," explained U Win. "Instead of celebrating birthdays with a party, they save their money and donate to the pagoda instead. Each gold plate on the upper stupa costs around eighteen hundred US dollars. The pagoda is so important to our people that they line up to donate gold plates. They take great pride in it.

"Shall we move on?" U Win called for the stray members of the group who had wandered off. "I will give you more information as we move around the courtyard."

At every turn, they found more statues of Buddha in prayer halls and pavilions—some made of marble, others of jade or the inevitable gold. Walls were lined with mirror tiles or marble and gold adornments. The majesty of the architecture was not lost on the Camera Club. Batteries were changed, memory cards swapped, and cameras whirred. Words could not describe this place adequately, so photos must.

Amanda had wandered ahead of the group, anxious to see around every corner. *I can't believe this place,* she was in awe.

U Win had a lot more information for the group. "The construction of each building is significant, as each part of it takes on spiritual meaning. For the main pagoda, they started with a mound-like structure that was based on the burial mounds of ascetics who were buried in a seated position. The stupa forms include bell shapes and even pyramid shapes.

"There is a large square plinth standing seven metres above the centre of the courtyard terrace. This raised platform supports smaller stupas. The four cardinal points — east, west, north, and south — are marked by four larger stupas, with another four medium-sized stupas at the corners of the plinth. Around this stand sixty-four small stupas, each donated by locals, each with its own jewel-topped spire. In front of these on the main terrace level, where we stand, is another row of sixty-four Buddha-filled pavilions interspersed with the eight planetary posts"

Hannah thought U Win made a great tour guide; he clearly loved his job. U Win's memory surpassed most men thirty years younger. "From the raised plinth, you see more octagonal terraces followed by five circular bands as the structure reaches into the sky. From there it resembles a bell topped by an upside down bowl.

Above this are the mouldings and then what we call the Lotus Petals. These are a band of downturned petals underneath another band of upturned petals. The final part of the stupa is called the banana bud before the jewelled hti on top.

"The pagoda structure has eight sides to commemorate the planetary posts," U Win recited. "The perimeter of the base is four hundred forty metres, with a height of just over a hundred metres. The central terrace measures two hundred seventy-five metres north to south and two hundred fifteen metres east to west. The main terrace is also home to several other pagodas, the largest of which is the Naungdawgyi. It is tiny in comparison to Shwedagon."

The group was introduced to the planetary posts, and U Win explained their importance. "There are eight planetary posts representing the eight days of the week. Wednesday is divided into morning and evening to be celebrated as two separate days. Locals pray at the station of their birth, and you can join in if you wish. If you don't know which day you were born, the almanacs provide the information for you. Please go to the fortune-tellers, and they will tell you. If you were born on Wednesday afternoon, the Rahu post standing at the northwest corner of the stupa is your planetary post."

Hannah was born on a Thursday, so she found her planetary post, stepped forward, lifted a bamboo cup to fill with water, and then poured the water over the head of the Buddha. This represented a wish for good fortune for the coming year, and others born on a Thursday did the same.

The group spent another two hours at the pagoda, joining thousands of others visiting today — pilgrims and monks, tourists and locals, all enjoying the spiritual centre of Myanmar.

On the way out, they stopped at the souvenir shops to buy boxed Buddhas or models of Shwedagon. Souvenirs were tucked into the bus along with the camera gear. The bus returned to the hotel for a dinner break.

"Please be ready to leave again promptly at eight o'clock tonight," advised Hannah. "We only have an hour tonight to catch some close-ups of the pagoda under lights before we meet again on the rooftop for some distance shots. If anyone cares to join us, Simon and I will be poolside for the next hour. Dinner is at six thirty. See you soon."

A quick change into swimsuits, and Hannah and her husband were racing down to the pool. The water was deliciously cool, glistening in the afternoon sun as they dove in and started to swim laps. They were both strong swimmers, but today was not the day to compete with each other over any distance. Swimming blew away the cobwebs of the day and was a great way to relax muscles that felt stale from sitting on the bus and walking on marbled tiles all day.

Nathan and Amanda were already baking in the sun, as Brits are prone to do anytime the temperature allows.

Jean-Pierre Claudens, a retired French doctor who saw himself as something of a playboy, was at the bar. He was chatting up Sophie Galena, the dark-haired Italian spinster from Bari. Jennifer Zweers, the overweight housewife from Hobart, was far more interested in Jean-Pierre than Sophie appeared to be. *The eternal triangle, it seems*, thought Hannah.

After half an hour in the water, Simon was ready for a beer. He and Ted propped up the bar while Hannah returned to the room to check her camera equipment. She called the front desk and asked for the catering department. "Hi, it's Hannah Nolan for the Global Camera Club. I just wanted to check that everything is ready for tonight. Yes, ten o'clock on the rooftop. Light canapés and drinks as per the menu I chose, that's right. Would you please make sure the lighting is candles only, so it does not reflect into the camera lens and photos? No, we won't need wait staff; thanks anyway."

Dinner was a two-course affair to speed up the process of getting everyone out the door on time. Hannah discouraged alcohol to ensure the night ran smoothly. There was no place for inebriation tonight.

The bus returned, and a young man stepped out to greet the group, his traditional longyi wrapped around his waist and a Western-style collared business shirt above it. He looked like a student.

"Good evening. I am Zaw, your guide for tonight's tour. U Win has asked me to take good care of you."

They again took their places on the bus and pulled out into the night traffic. The sky was black, and Shwedagon dominated the skyline even from a distance. A golden aura emanated from Singuttara Hill, where Shwedagon was now illuminated for all to admire.

The streets were still busy, but peak hour had clearly passed. Within minutes, the bus pulled into the southern entrance. It looked familiar but was marginally different from the eastern entrance they had gone through earlier in the day. Even with fewer steps to the main terrace than they'd encountered earlier in the day, it was easier to opt for the elevator again. Shoes and socks were relinquished to the storage racks once more.

The elevator door opened, and the entire group squeezed into the limited space to ascend to the main terrace. As they exited the walkway back onto the marble terrace courtyard, they encountered one of the bodhi trees planted on the main deck.

Zaw told them, "The bodhi tree is deemed to be the Tree of Life. It has a long association with Buddha, who was believed to be reclining under a bodhi tree when he received enlightenment. Every tree here on the main terrace is watered by hand."

Shwedagon glowed above them, and spotlights focused on different parts of the structure, sending a glow into the night. The smaller pavilions were peaceful, and the planetary stations fairly quiet with only a few visitors still pouring water over the head of one Buddha or another.

The atmosphere was at once spectacular, yet different from the afternoon experience. "It is truly majestic," Hannah said to Simon, "yet these evening lights don't do justice to the intricate carvings we could see in the daylight. There is more serenity tonight, though, more solitude."

The crowds had thinned, yet there were still plenty of people wandering around or entering prayer halls. Some picnicked on the cool marble under foot. The complex closed at 10:00 p.m. The lights would stay on all night until the complex opened again at 4:00 a.m. Foreigners were not admitted before 6:00 a.m. But on the Waxing Day of Tabaung in March and the Waxing Day of Wakhaung that marks the beginning of Buddhist Lent in June, the pagoda would be open for a full twenty-four hours.

They again walked clockwise, in the Buddhist way, noticing many buildings in the evening light that were inconspicuous in daylight. An hour later they had captured their photos, soon to be compared to the daytime pictures. It was time to leave, yet they still had the distance shots to capture from the hotel before the day was done. They reluctantly headed back to the bus. Shwedagon left an indelible imprint on their psyche.

Hannah realized she has seen no security cameras anywhere on the main terrace. This would be a blessing, given her criminal intent.

9

CRIMINAL INTENT

At ten o'clock, the last members of the Camera Club arrived on the rooftop terrace of the Summit Parkview hotel in downtown Yangon. The setting was perfect for a warm evening. Candles decorated the floor, and the low tables were set with white cloths. The light evening breeze made the candles flicker. The night was quiet, and the group's voices hushed. There was an air of serious anticipation.

Supper was ready on a long table on the side of the terrace, with drinks chilling in buckets of ice. Camera cases littered the large rooftop terrace. While the club members opened their cases and began assembling their gear, Hannah moved through the group, giving instructions and advice where needed.

Simon stood at the edge of the roof terrace, looking down over the pool below, enjoying the canapés and cold beer, his task for the evening complete. Having carried Hannah's cases to the rooftop, he was now off the hook. All around him, cameras were aimed directly at Shwedagon, aglow on the hill nearby.

After about twenty minutes, Amanda excused herself from the group, happy to leave Nathan to play with his camera. Simon also made his excuses.

"I'll just give Amanda a police escort home" he declared. Simon knew from experience that the group would now "get all technical." Hannah would take the group through a number of different camera effects and settings, working with each person in turn. It would take at least another hour.

Hannah knew he was just looking for an excuse to escape to his bed. She kissed him goodnight and watched him leave.

"Right," said Hannah. "Are we ready?"

Faces beamed back at her as Molly spoke for the group: "Let's do it!"

Hannah walked over to the door that led back down to the hotel. She leaned forward and locked it. No one could disturb them now. She was thankful that Simon would not question how long she would be gone from their room tonight. He'd be sleeping like a babe!

One by one, the drones came out. Most were fairly small but capable of covering the distance between the hotel and Shwedagon. There was a flurry of activity as drone components were extracted from their cases and clipped together and settings were tested. Cameras were mounted into the dedicated slots and clipped into place, and settings were checked with Hannah.

Each group member checked the sightings through the camera viewfinder. They needed to understand exactly what to look for on their iPads. They would be driving the drones from the computers, and a high level of precision would be needed. Lasers were checked and retractor grips tightened.

Hannah's drone was the largest and most customized; her target was the most important. Her octocopter had been fitted with GPS-assisted flight controls. These would be paramount to success tonight. It had been specifically adapted to allow her to control it alone. A powerful laser cutter had been added to one of the drone's tripod legs, a retractor grip fitted into another leg, and an extendable basket fitted to the third.

She opened the octocopter's case and carefully lifted the component parts from the foam lining. Hannah went through the checklist: propellers locked in, check; failsafe return to base turned on, check; AV downlink to computer, check; flight batteries fully charged, check. It took just three minutes for the larger drone to be operational.

One by one, the others signalled that they were ready. Hannah handed them their assigned GPS locations. Each GPS co-ordinate representing the location of a jewel-topped spire around the perimeter of Shwedagon. Digby had carefully recorded each of these today on their first visit to the pagoda. Each one of them would try to retrieve gemstones from at least three spires around the main terrace.

The first drone lifted off effortlessly, closely followed by the others. They looked like giant black locusts in the night sky, swarming together toward the same goal. Their gentle buzzing sounds were muted by the traffic below.

Hannah had chosen this hotel, in part, because all the lighting on the roof was aimed down toward the ground. The drones would only be exposed when they were over Singuttara Hill. The site was closed, and security guards did not patrol the main terrace. There were no security cameras on site, and any on nearby buildings would be aimed at the ground, not at the sky around the pagoda.

They were careful to keep the drones just under the designated global height restriction of 120 metres. As they approached Shwedagon, the drones headed in different directions. Each drone flew over the terrace and around the pagoda according to the GPS locations that Hannah had worked out for each club member.

The drones were kept well apart so there would be no chance they might interfere with each other. No sense getting too close to your team member.

The lasers were deployed, and the fine laser cutting blade extended from each drone. One by one, they honed in on the top of their assigned spire. They hovered while the retractor grip slipped around each gemstone. The cutters made quick work of slicing through the soft gold settings that encased each gem. The drones lifted away.

It took less than a minute to separate each gem from the spire. The drones headed back to the hotel roof to deposit their prizes before returning for another until they had captured every target.

Hannah's octocopter was the last to lift off from the hotel, rising like a giant spider in the sky, but it covered the distance to Shwedagon faster than the smaller drones. Just minutes after taking flight, her drone was hovering around the bell shape of the pagoda. Hannah had more difficulty keeping the drone out of sight as it climbed the height of the main spire. The hairs on her neck stood up with nervous anticipation. Fine beads of perspiration glowed on her forehead in the moonlight.

Her iPad screen showed gold and more gold: the pagoda was even more resplendent up close. Slowly the drone ascended, Hannah keeping it steady as it climbed ever higher.

As the drone lifted above the banana bud and then the hti, Hannah felt instantly greedy at the sight of the gold and silver bells. Her mouth was dry by the time the majestic vane came into sight.

"Oh shit! Look at that!" she muttered. The vane was dripping with gemstones embedded in gold.

The giant "spider" climbed higher until the pagoda's orb filled the viewfinder. "Oh my God, that is heaven!" Hannah couldn't help herself; desire coursed through every bone in her body. *Why is it that you can't have what you want most? If only it weren't so heavy!* There was no drone in the world that could lift that weight off the spire.

The orb was a picture of regal embellishment — royal fortunes long ago spent on a temple decoration. *Unbelievable.* The gemstones flickered in the spotlights far beneath the drone. Hannah could see the diamonds, all eighteen hundred carats of them set in real gold. *Bloody hell!*

Higher still, the drone crept up the spire. As it climbed above the orb, Hannah got her first glimpse of the Shwedagon Diamond.

"WOW!" she whispered.

At the apex of the orb, the diamond was embedded in the top of the golden sphere. Around it was set a multitude of smaller diamonds, then a braid of gold "rope" that formed a pyramid shape above the main gem.

Quickly assessing the shape and location of the Shwedagon diamond, Hannah decided she would need to cut through the gold braid first. She turned on her drone's laser light, its beam instantly green against the diamond. There was a flash of reflection from the seventy-six-carat stone. Hannah hoped the flash of light had not been seen from anywhere nearby — but then, the danger was most of the fun.

It took only seconds to cut through the soft gold braid, the pieces falling down the side of the pagoda. Hannah gasped as she saw these pieces of gold hit the bells around the "umbrella" high above the main platform, and breathed a sigh of relief to see that nobody came running at the sound.

She carefully deployed the retractor grip and manoeuvred it over the setting that held the massive diamond. The grip's "hand" settled securely around the bulk of the gem, much of which had been buried in the gold setting for 150 years.

The wind had come up and was growing stronger on the hill. The drone wobbled but Hannah was able to steady it. Circling the drone around the gemstone, she used the laser to cut through the base of the setting. The retractor grip held tight. Finally the gemstone and its gold setting were separated from the spire. Hannah exhaled slowly.

The drone backed away and the basket extending from the tripod leg opened to take its prize. The retractor grip lowered the diamond into the basket before releasing its grip. It could not have been easier to steal the Shwedagon Diamond.

Hannah backed the drone away from the main spire and started to drop some of its height. The moment was filled with excited achievement. Adrenaline rushed through her veins, her pulse had been racing without her realising. *Calm down, breathe slowly now.*

The smile had grown wide on her face. She started to turn the drone around to head back to her. Beneath her feet, the building shuddered.

"What the…"

Birds screeched swiftly out of nearby trees. The skies above the People's Park opposite were suddenly filled with birds scurrying away from their night-time habitats. The ground rumbled and Hannah almost lost her balance. She recognized the distinct trembling of an earthquake. Hannah grabbed the side wall of the roof terrace as the building swayed beneath her feet.

"Oh fu…" cried timid little Sophie Galena. The men tried to steady the tables, the women, and their drones all at once.

As Hannah stumbled, so did the drone. She had to steady it quickly or risk losing the contents of the basket. The drone had nearly eight hundred metres still to cover before landing on the rooftop.

With the first set of gemstones safely returned to the hotel roof top, the others had swapped their drone batteries for fresh ones. The swarm of mechanical cicadas had just lifted back into the air heading for Shwedagon once more. They were all thrown off balance. There was a struggle to control their drones in flight.

There was another rumbling and they watched as the surface of Ahlone Road opened up in front of the hotel. The crack formed quickly, until it covered nearly thirty metres along the tarmac. A lamppost cracked and fell to the ground. Cars skidded to a halt, unsure how to react to the earth moving beneath them. Car alarms screeched into the night, triggered by the tremors beneath the parked vehicles.

Inside the park trees disappeared into a massive sink hole that suddenly opened up. Elephant Fountain cracked, sending water spewing high into the night sky. The stage of the Festival grounds broke in two, one side jutting a metre higher than the other.

Next door, the Yangon International Hotel started to show cracks down its eastern face. People came scurrying out into the street.

"Keep calm!" Hannah shouted. "Bring the drones back so we can get out of here!"

The disappointment was palpable. With only some of the gemstones secured in the first run, there were so many more left behind. They would have to leave them.

Hannah struggled to steady her drone as the next tremor hit the building. The octocopter closed the distance to the hotel. Amid birds struggling to escape the tremors, the drone was finally brought home with the "return to base failsafe" deployed.

The drone landed alongside her, and Hannah had her first glimpse of the famous diamond. It was massive. The gold setting would be removed later to free the diamond. She swept the gem into her hand and deposited it in her camera case. The drone was quickly dismantled; the components packed away. There was no time to lose.

The others, with shaking hands and rattled nerves, scrambled to get their drones and cameras packed down and into cases, the gemstones stuffed inside. Aaron was the first at the door to the stairwell. He grabbed the handle and pulled. The door would not open. "It's jammed!" he yelled.

"It's locked!" Hannah yelled back. Aaron flipped the deadbolt lever to open, but the door still wouldn't budge.

"It's really jammed!" he shouted.

The others were quickly behind him. First Ted and then Digby tried pulling on the door. Nothing. Panic was starting to set in.

"Shit," said Ted. "It must have been pushed out of alignment. What are we going to do?"

Hannah could hear Sophie sobbing behind her.

Laura was on her mobile phone, trying to contact hotel reception. There was a sudden loud crash from the stairwell and Simon came plummeting through the doorway.

"Are you OK?" He was out of breath and looking around for Hannah. "I got thrown out of bed. Hell of a way to wake up!"

"Oh, Simon. Thank God you thought to come and get us!" As eager as Hannah had been for Simon to leave earlier in the evening, she was even more relieved to see him now.

Nathan rushed past to go in search of Amanda, nervous for what she had experienced on her own throughout the earthquake. He found her cowering under the desk, crying uncontrollably. "Where were you?" she cried when Nathan charged into the room. He hugged his bride and led her down to join the others outside the hotel.

Within minutes the group had moved their gear off the rooftop and down to the parking lot. They were thankful the hotel was only six stories. The quake had subsided, but the area showed a lot of damage. Emergency services started to arrive; police were directing traffic away from the area.

The hotel manager appeared, announcing to the assembled crowd, "Please stay calm. We have engineers on their way to assess the hotel, but we seem to have escaped any significant damage. As soon as we get clearance, we can let you back into your rooms. In the meantime, we are setting up drinks over there. Please help yourselves with our compliments."

The gathered crowd started to settle. The activity around them was enough to distract them. Sirens howled in the background as emergency vehicles raced across the city.

Nathan Richardson was the first to notice the groaning sound in the distance. He turned toward Singuttara Hill, drawn by the sound of an almighty crack growing into a massive growl. The young man watched as the whole top of the pagoda cracked then crashed downward. The top of Shwedagon was gone, from the banana bud upward. "Look at Shwedagon!" he cried.

Heads turned, not knowing what they were looking for.

Hannah grabbed her camera. The shutter raced as it captured three images every second. Aaron had started to unpack her drone for her. He and Ted reassembled it quickly as Hannah worked her camera. This had to be captured.

Even from this distance, it was obvious. The zoom function in the camera confirmed it.

Every member of the group stared open-mouthed toward Shwedagon. The top of the spire was missing. There was no "umbrella" to be seen. That meant that everything above it, had come crashing down. The hti, the vane, and the orb were gone.

In the midst of this disaster, Hannah was instantly pleased—nobody would know the gems were missing. It could take them weeks, maybe months to discover their loss.

10

DESTRUCTION

Outside the pagoda, monks were uncharacteristically hurrying across the road from their hostel nearby. They had known there was a problem when they heard the massive crack from the hill above them. Aftershocks had continued to hit Singuttara Hill.

Their robes were flying behind them as they neared the stairway of the southern approach to Shwedagon. Some lights were still somehow shining, and they could see the damage before they reached it. Debris had fallen in every direction, the stairs cracked, decorations peeled from walls and ceiling panels dangled from above.

The elevator was wedged at an angle between floors. Palm trees leaned against the exterior wall blocking the entrance to the elevator shaft.

Other nearby residents joined the monks. Mobile phones screeched for attention as news went out of damage from the quake. Sirens screamed in the background. Voices trilled through the growing crowd.

A policeman arrived and joined an older monk. They started their ascent toward the main platform, picking their way through the debris. Bricks littered the steps, impeding their progress. Gingerly, they found their footing on each stair tread, climbing slowly higher.

The handrail had detached from the wall, protruding sharply into the space ahead of them, leaving them little to hold onto as they inched gingerly upward. Water gushed down the steps on one side of the stairs, escaping out of a crack in the wall onto the hillside beneath them.

The main marble terrace was within sight when they realised there was an obstruction ahead of them. In the half light of early morning, they recognised the shape of a small stupa, toppled over and blocking their way. They climbed under the edge of the stupa, and scrambled onto the marble terrace.

They stood, stunned at the destruction. It looked like a building site with a mangle of materials in every direction. In front of the stairs, the pavilions on either side had cracked and slipped off their foundations, giving the policeman the strange impression of drunks in a bar.

All around them, structures lay on their side. One large Buddha had fallen face first into the prayer hall. The pavilion of the Saedawmu Buddha showed cracked walls. This wish-fulfilling Buddha would be out of action for a while. His face lay shattered on the floor.

A nearby bodhi tree had been uprooted and rested against three golden stupas. Farther on, more stupas littered the terrace. Prayer halls had Buddhas resting against each other like drunken soldiers. An orgy of Buddhas lay strewn across the terrace floor.

The planetary post for Wednesday leaned precariously on the small wall in front of them — the only thing stopping them from falling onto the terrace.

Jade Buddha reclined on his back inside his pavilion.

Walking through water streaming across the marble, they picked their way clockwise. Passing Saturday corner, they saw the statue of King Sakka had fallen off his perch. The "lotus petal" pedestal had cracked and partially swallowed the king's statue, now sitting in the flower rather than on it.

As they approached the western walkway, they saw something glittering in the moonlight but weren't sure what they were seeing.

Above them, the vane was wedged into the side of the pagoda, about a third of the way up. Like a broken rib, it stuck out from the wall of the bell shape. Its massive weight had firmly implanted it into the gold structure that once supported it.

When the vane broke away, it snapped the orb off its support. The orb had crashed down the side of the pagoda, bouncing off the edged terraces at its base, crushing the small stupas in front of it. It had rolled through the melee of buildings and bounced forward until it finally stopped on the main terrace near the western walkway. They found it sitting in its own crater on the outer terrace.

The diamonds from the orb were lying sprinkled like fairy dust across the marble tiles. Many of the gems had been washed away and might never be recovered. The orb was badly dented from its many contact points on its downward spiral. This was the source of the glittering sparkle they had seen from a distance.

As they approached Thursday's planetary post, the policeman heard a sound like a slot machine jackpot. Coins rippled from the ATM onto the floor. Farther on, they came to King Singu's bell lying on the ground. Its twenty-four tons had left a massive indentation in the floor.

They didn't need to see any more. It was obvious there had been significant damage to this sacred site. The policeman called his headquarters to report the damage. He had asked them to find someone to turn off the water.

Before the policeman could end his call, the monk asked him to provide officers to secure the main walkway entrances until morning. The pagoda's governing committee would close the site, and arrange a massive clean-up. It would take weeks; reconstruction would take months.

The sun was starting to peek over the eastern horizon. They continued on toward the northern entrance. It was too dangerous to finish the tour of the terrace in the half light of early morning.

They made their exit through the northern stairs. The damage here was just as extensive as the southern stairwell. On their way back down to the parking lot, the monk told of seeing a swarm of enormous black locusts and the glint of green lights earlier in the evening.

"Really? When was this?" the policeman asked, pulling out his notebook.

"Just before the earthquake hit. It was Buddha's warning."

11

OBSTRUCTION

Hannah's camera was once again clipped into the drone. It was aloft almost instantly, this time to capture photos of the damage caused by the quake.

By the time the drone returned twenty minutes later, the engineers had arrived at the hotel. While they were inside inspecting the hotel for damage, the group were huddled around Hannah's iPad. The photos of the devastation were shocking.

Many of the smaller pavilions had been ripped from their stands; planetary posts lay crumbled around the main terrace. Giant Buddhas were on their side. Burst water pipes had sent flooding waters across the marble floors. Gold plates had slid from the structure above, smashing through delicate lacework and gilded decorations around the perimeter.

The scene was eerie in its contrast to the pagoda they had visited twice today.

It was hours before the hotel was given the all clear. As they entered the lobby, they saw chandeliers lying smashed on the floor. In the nearby bar, bottles had sprung off the shelves and now littered the area. Liquid stained the carpet; glass fragments were everywhere.

In the library, books had flown off shelves. The fax machine had fallen off a desk in the business centre. Thankfully, there was no structural damage. The same could not be said for the International Hotel next door. It seemed to have taken the brunt of the shockwave in the area. Its guests, still in pyjamas, were being loaded onto buses to be dispersed to other accommodation.

"Are you sure it's O.K. to use the elevators?" Gordon asked. The hotel manager assured him that the engineers had declared them to be safe.

Nobody got much sleep; a mixture of adrenaline and fear made sure of that. But they gave the minibars a workout, with no thought for the cost.

In the morning, a simple breakfast was served. The kitchen was in disarray and only one electric hotplate was working. Nobody complained about the bread and jam, as long as they could have a warm cup of tea.

The bus arrived at eight o'clock. "Is everyone all right?" U Win was genuinely concerned.

"Yes, thank you," Hannah responded. "What about your family?"

"We live to the north of town, away from the centre of the quake, so not much damage to report." U Win was taking control of the group to ensure they were kept calm. "I have some news."

Eyes turned expectantly toward him, brows furrowed.

"We cannot get to Bago; it was the epicentre of the quake. The roads are badly affected right around Yangon," he started to explain. "Instead we are taking you back to the port."

Shoulders shrugged their understanding of the change in plans.

"We are just waiting for the ship to return," he continued.

"For the what?" Simon asked.

"Last night, when the quake struck, there was concern that it could cause a tsunami in the ocean." U Win was trying to placate the group. "The river is exposed to the sea, and the ship was in danger of being grounded if a tsunami hit. All the ships had to go out to sea."

"So when will it come back, or will it come back?" It was Jonathan Beadle, a retired lawyer who was used to asking questions.

U Win said, "We have had word this morning that the *Quest* is on its way back up the river now. It expects to be dockside in two hours. We have instructions to return all passengers at once for an immediate departure. Sadly, your visit is being cut short."

"What about the roads back to the port?" Simon asked.

"They are somewhat damaged. It will take some time to get you back to the vessel."

There were sighs all around as the reality of their situation sank in.

"Please, collect all your belongings and have them ready for the porters to bring down to the bus. We leave in fifteen minutes," U Win informed them.

"Somewhat damaged" had been an understatement. Traffic was a nightmare. There was more damage in the outlying areas than downtown. The long bridge into Yangon was intact and had been cleared by the military engineers early that morning. Without the bridge, there would only have been the railway to get them out of Yangon, and work crews were still walking the track, checking for damage. Villages were in turmoil and progress was slow. There was no police escort this time. They were too busy elsewhere.

There was less damage closer to the port. It appeared the bus would manage to get through. They had been on the bus for nearly five hours before the port cranes came into view. The *Quest* sat waiting for them.

The car carrier had left the port the day before, so the dock was now deserted except for the *Quest*. There was an eerie silence. Nothing was moving in the port: no cars, no trucks, no people. The security gates were still manned, but it was only the buses that passed through.

Theirs was not the last bus to arrive; there were two more still in transit. The group unloaded their gear onto the trolleys to be taken back on board.

The group members each thanked U Win, shaking his hand and sliding tips into his palm. Their visit to Yangon would not easily be forgotten.

At the top of the gangway, ship security scanned identity cards and directed all bags and cases to the x-ray machine. This was the moment of truth. The camera gear and drones had been scanned back onto the ship several times over the last few days. Would the additional contents be questioned?

Hannah knew that because diamonds were essentially carbon, they could show up under x-rays, and this particular diamond was encased in gold. Would the metal trigger enquiry from security? She felt a thin layer of sweat appear on her palms.

Behind her, Jean-Pierre carried a water bottle with his right hand cupped around the bottom. Inside the bottle, swishing around in the water, was a three-carat diamond.

Jean-Pierre had managed to remove the diamond from its setting before concealing it in the water bottle. He had often come back on board with a water bottle in his hand and knew that he would just be waved through. Nobody worried about checking a water bottle. He just had to hold the bottle still enough so that the diamond did not tap against the sides. He did not want to draw attention to the bottle. He passed through the metal scanners unchecked.

Next to him security guards lifted the overnight bags onto the conveyor belt first. The bags disappeared behind the black rubber curtains to be inspected under x-ray.

"What's this?" asked the head of security, whose eyes were on the scanner. He backed up the conveyor belt and withdrew a gift box from one of the overnight bags. He opened it to reveal a large emerald in a golden setting.

"Just a replica I bought at the markets," Laura Glenn lied. "There's another box with a Buddha in it. Would you like to see?"

"No, that's fine." Security waved the bag through and then ignored all the others with gift boxes inside them.

The camera cases slid through without question about the metal content; the drone cases followed. It seemed that getting the drones out of the country would be a lot easier than getting them in! The group collected their gear and walked away.

Hannah stowed her cases in her stateroom and headed for the bar with Simon. Champagne was pointless — she was allergic to it!

Two hours later, with the last of the passengers back on board, the *Quest* slipped away from the dock and sailed downriver toward Thailand.

The Shwedagon Diamond was on board.

12

SEA DAY

An extra day at sea had proved to be a bonus for the Camera Club. After sailing from Yangon the previous night, the group had agreed to spend the day being pampered.

The girls had booked in for spa treatments. The guys had opted for massages or the Japanese bath house experience.

Hannah was the first to arrive at the salon. She dropped her oversized handbag onto the floor alongside the treatment chair. A hand massage and manicure was long overdue. She settled into the chair and smiled at the attendant.

Amanda Donaldson was just behind her and was taken to the basin for a shampoo and blow-dry. As a hairdresser with her own salon back in Portsmouth, it wasn't often that Amanda had someone else do her hair for her. She was looking forward to this morning's pampering after the events of the last few days.

Laura Glenn and Maggie Hooper arrived next. They were ushered into the chairs on either side of Hannah. As they greeted her with a kiss on the cheek, Maggie bent forward and discreetly dropped a small wrapped parcel into Hannah's handbag.

Another fifteen minutes passed before Molly Johns arrived. She greeted Hannah with a peck on the cheek and dropped a small parcel into Hannah's open bag. Molly moved to the hairdresser's chair for a tint to be applied. By the time Hannah's manicure was finished, Sophie Galena and Jennifer Zweers were arriving. The greeting ritual was repeated as donations were made to the handbag. Sophie took Laura's chair next to Hannah when Laura moved to the foot bath. Jennifer slid into a lounge chair to wait her turn.

Hannah's pedicure began, as the ladies from Noosa arrived. Janet Richards and Brenda Cox were incredibly fit. They had met while competing in "Iron Woman" events. Within weeks they were cohabiting.

Hannah looked like the most popular woman on board as the greetings continued. Unnoticed by the attendants, Hannah's handbag was being filled. There was a lot of small talk among the group. It helped to lighten the mood. Tensions were high, and would stay high until they flew home from Singapore.

Hilary Swanston was running late. She greeted Hannah and dropped her contribution into the bag on the floor. She slumped into the chair left empty by Jennifer.

Marjan Christiane arrived for a colour and cut, greeted Hannah and moved to the waiting area. Her arrival signalled the last of the females of the group.

Hannah's handbag was getting heavy.

She enjoyed being among friends who liked a challenge. They also liked being rewarded for taking risks.

When she was done, Hannah said good-bye to the members of the group and then signed for her treatments. The charge would appear on her stateroom account within minutes.

Hannah hoisted her handbag onto her shoulder, careful not to grimace at the weight. She was thankful that she was used to lifting her heavy camera cases. She needed extra muscle to lift the handbag now. It was noticeably heavier with the contributions inside.

This was only part of the spoils; the men still had the rest of the loot. The couples had split the chore between them. Each couple had to decide who would deliver the gems to either Hannah or Jean-Pierre.

Meanwhile, the men had started to gather. Jean-Pierre had finished his morning workout, showered, and was now on the massage table, face down. His gym bag was on the floor under the edge of the table. He was waiting for the masseuse to return when Nathan Donaldson called a greeting as he walked past the open door.

Ted Glenn entered the massage room, walked over to Jean-Pierre and slapped him on the back as a greeting. Ted leaned forward and placed two small wrapped parcels into the gym bag under the table, his own and Nathan's donations.

A small procession of men repeated the greeting, mirroring the women's movements in the salon. Anders Christiane and Digby Tennyson arrived early. Contributions were made to the gym bag as greetings were offered to Jean-Pierre. The pair moved off in the direction of the bath house.

Jock McAdams and Gordon McTaggart were looking forward to the Japanese bath. They greeted Jean-Pierre with a smack on the bum. It was just too tempting! He grunted at their antics, and watched as their donation was made to the gym bag.

Aaron Swanston, Philip Ngu, and Jonathan Beadle had opted for massages. They arrived in the treatment room and greeted Jean-Pierre, dropping the last of the gemstones into the gym bag. The conversation turned to football and microbrews just as the masseuse returned.

Hannah's handbag was sitting on her bed. She had returned to her cabin to wait for word from Jean-Pierre, who had agreed to let her know when he was back in his cabin.

Hannah was in the bathroom when she heard Simon return from his tanning session.

"That you love?" Simon called as he heard the water taps being turned off.

"Yes, silly. Who else would it be?" Hannah opened the bathroom door, to see Simon reaching out to her handbag

"Do you have tweezers, Hannah? I've got a splinter in my hand." Simon was oblivious to the rapid footsteps behind him.

"I'll get them, Si!" Hannah pushed his hand gently away from the bag. She steered Simon toward the bedside chest of drawers. "They're in the first aid bag over here."

Jean-Pierre had returned from his massage. His shoulder was a little sore from lifting the weight of the gym bag.

Oh, the price you pay! He thought.

He was waiting for Hannah to deliver the rest of the kitty to him. The settings of gold had to be removed from each gemstone, and the French doctor had been assigned that task. He already had the Shwedagon

Diamond and had massaged it from its gold coat overnight. Jean-Pierre had been surprised to discover it
was in a setting that was heavily encrusted with smaller
diamonds. He had counted fifty seven stones hugging
the Shwedagon diamond. They would become a nice
addition to the kitty.

The heavy gym bag was on the desk when Hannah
knocked on his cabin door. No words were exchanged
as she stepped inside. Hannah removed the morning's
donations from her handbag and placed them on the
desk top. She smiled, winked at Jean-Pierre, and slid
quietly back out of the room. No more than thirty seconds had elapsed.

Jean-Pierre was a retired surgeon from Chantilly,
just outside Paris, and his fingers were nimble and agile. He was used to performing delicate work; his ability to separate gold from gems was second to none. He
had become a valuable asset to the Camera Club.

Jean-Pierre set to work. First, he assessed each gemstone in its gold setting for size and then sorted them
along his workspace. The task would be tedious and
lengthy. It would require him to work long into the
night. Only when the gems were packed securely into
the cabin's safe would he succumb to ordering some
dinner.

Surgeons need an escape from their everyday lives,
a hobby to take their minds off the serious nature of
their work. Jean-Pierre had learned to play the violin
and then chosen another hobby. Long ago, he had

started hiking in the mountains on weekends. He was with friends when they stumbled across some raw emeralds. Jean-Pierre was instantly hooked on gemstones and pursued gemology as his next hobby. He had learned to shape various settings to secure a gemstone in place. That meant he also knew how to deconstruct them.

These stones were different because they were not simple rings and pendants. Each stone had been set at the apex of a spire; their gold coats anchoring them in place against wind and rain. The settings were fairly crude to Jean-Pierre's trained eye. As always, great care would be needed to ensure the stones were not damaged or scarred in the process.

He took advantage of the heating element from the cabin's hairdryer. It soon became his main tool in separating the stones from the gold. His other tools were secreted in his Gladstone bag; it accompanied the doctor on every journey.

One by one, he freed the stones, placing them in one pile and the gold in another.

Gold was a problem. A nice problem, but still a problem. Gold is notoriously heavy even in small amounts. It would have to be taken off the ship in small quantities. It did not matter that the gold was now in broken shards — it would eventually be melted down and sold separately.

Hannah had lined up a contact to buy the gold. Jean-Pierre was to deliver it in three consignments.

The first delivery was scheduled for Phuket. The others were due in Langkawi and then Port Klang, on consecutive days of the voyage. The ship's itinerary made it easy to arrange this to coincide with the port days.

In less than one day, the ship would arrive into Phuket. Jean-Pierre worked all day and long into the night. By breakfast time, he had to return the Shwedagon Diamond and other gemstones to Hannah.

13

PHUKET

"This is an announcement from Customer Services. Local authorities have now cleared us for landing. We will begin the tender-boat service shortly. Please proceed to Level Three to join the next available tender."

There was no dock on this side of Phuket Island. The *Quest* was anchored in the bay nearly three kilometres off shore. Hannah grabbed photos of the headlands on either side of the ship. As the sun climbed into the sky, the heat was already apparent. The anchor had been dropped in an area that was immensely peaceful. Small yachts sailed in the distance, farther out to sea.

The headland on the southern side of the vessel was covered with dense forest. As the ship moved around it and farther into the bay, a small, sandy beach appeared. Little houses were dotted above it. Palm trees swayed gently in the morning breeze. It was a perfect scene — all that Hannah had imagined this tropical island would be.

On the other side of the ship, the northern headland showed lots of building sites climbing the hillsides. Hotel villas were tucked into the trees above quiet little coves. Many resorts dominated the scenery on this side of the bay. Beautiful white sandy beaches dotted every bay along the headland.

Patong Beach, the main beach and the main tourist drag in Phuket, was in front of the ship. In the center of the picture, a single high-rise — possibly thirty stories high — towered over the landscape. The apartment buildings on either side were just eight stories, so it looked monstrous in comparison.

Patong Beach was long — a couple of kilometres from one end to the other. The central part of the beach was crowded — hundreds of people were already sunning themselves — although it was not yet nine in the morning. The far ends of the beach were quieter, with just a few stragglers strolling along the waterside. Boats were tied up close to shore ready for tourist day trips.

A road over the hillside delivered vehicles onto the main beach strip. Cars lined the waterfront road. The main township sat behind the beach. The southern end of the beach, where the tenders delivered passengers onto the pier, was fairly quiet.

Jean-Pierre was on one of the first tenders leaving the *Quest*. He would be happy to get this part over and done with early today. The weight in his backpack was cutting into his shoulders. When he disembarked the tender with his backpack firmly in place, he headed for the taxi rank.

"The Diamond Cottage Resort at Karon Beach, please, driver." He settled into the back seat for the twenty-five-minute ride.

Jean-Pierre found it quite amusing that the contact had picked this location as the meeting point. How could he have known the significance of meeting at a resort named the Diamond?

Built in Thai style, the resort nestled in the hills between Karon and Kata Beach. There was a feeling of exotic beauty here among the guestrooms and villas of Diamond Cottage resort.

Jean-Pierre headed to the Ma Prow restaurant to meet his contact over a late breakfast.

An older gentleman was waiting at a table in the far corner. As always, he was well dressed and exuded an air of confidence. He rose to meet the French doctor, and smiled a greeting.

Jean-Pierre extended his hand to his old friend. They had met by chance in Bordeaux years before, and the friendship developed from there.

"How are you, *mon ami*?" Jean-Pierre said, as he placed the backpack under the edge of the table alongside his friend's chair.

"Well, thank you. Pleased to be able to meet you before the day gets hot." The older man had given nothing away to anyone who might have overheard the conversation. Small talk ensued as breakfast was ordered, delivered, and consumed.

An hour later, Jean-Pierre rose from the table. His friend picked up the bill, lifted the backpack onto his shoulder, and extended a handshake to the French doctor. "Shall we do this again in Langkawi tomorrow?"

As the morning wore on, the sea started to get choppy from a sea breeze whipping across the bay. The tender ride into the beach was rough. Hannah stumbled at the edge of the tender as she disembarked. Her bag started to slip from her hand and she nearly dropped it into the water. Snatching it up before it disappeared into the water, Simon rescued it. Hannah smiled her thanks — more than he would ever know.

She followed the others along the jetty toward the beach. Her nerves were showing; the final stage was always the hardest, surprisingly. The pressure was off and she could start to relax, but keeping her emotions in check was proving difficult.

Today the focus was on fencing the gemstones.

Getting the diamond off the ship had been easy. It was simply a case of walking off the ship with it. Security didn't check bags as passengers left the ship, only when they came back.

Thai authorities were not dockside to check bags. Most countries seemed to be more concerned with cruise passengers bringing fresh fruit ashore. Disease carried by fresh fruits and vegetables could ruin local crops.

It was a long walk along the beach to meet the tour bus. Patong, the main beach in Phuket, was a long clean sandy beach with plenty of dappled shade from the palm trees. Hannah thought it would be a great place to spend the day. She watched Jet Skis weave in and out of swimmers in the water, which struck her as more than a little dangerous. Parachutes floated above speed boats close to shore. She observed the varieties of red tones on the sunburned bodies lying on the sand, and was convinced there would always be plenty of worshippers of sun, sea and sand here on Patong Beach.

The main tourist drag was a thriving place with shops, bars, restaurants, and hotels. Every imaginable nationality seemed to be represented among the tourists. Hannah heard various European accents intermingled with Asian languages and American drawls. She had heard that a walk through town would reveal a preponderance of girlie bars among the restaurants and slightly sleazy retail stores, but that was not the direction they were going.

They spotted the bus stop outside a tourist kiosk halfway along the beach. Buses were lined up to accept passengers from the ship. Within minutes, they started to pull out into the traffic for a tour around the island.

Simon was horrified to notice the wiring along the way. Thousands of wires were strung haphazardly, many trailing down to street level. Metal light poles showed exposed wires within. "Remind me not to touch anything, will you love?" he said, with a humourless laugh. "Geez, I thought Ireland was bad, but this takes the cake!"

The drive around the island was picturesque and provided lots of opportunities for Hannah to capture photos. The island was a myriad of resorts, beaches, little villages, and coves. The water was clear and blue, beaches clean and uncrowded. Roadside lampposts were topped with traditional sculptures that looked like flying dragons swinging lanterns from their beaks.

"I'm glad I brought extra memory sticks." Hannah told Simon, as her camera got another workout.

She spotted a giant Buddha high on a hilltop, overlooking the villages and farms beneath it. Its whole body glimmered in the sunlight; it seemed to be carved from white marble.

Religion was clearly an important part of local life. There were many different styles of temples in Thailand, including Chinese temples with rainbow-coloured dragons wrapped around pillars, and Thai temples with whitewashed walls and rooftop corners turned up to the sky.

Their tour guide warned them that each temple had a brick outbuilding for storing fireworks — in an important part of worshipping in Thailand. The sounds of firecrackers reverberated around the temple grounds, frightening the unprepared.

Farmlets took over as they wandered out of town toward the centre of the island, where they passed the Phuket Heroines Monument. Folklore told of two women, Chan and Mook, who dressed as men to save Phuket from invading Burmese armies in 1785. Here they were, captured in bronze and bedecked in fresh flowers in the middle of a roundabout on Thepkasattri Road.

Soon they arrived at the cashew nut farm, in the central hills. The trees were not currently in fruit, so they were disappointed to miss seeing the fruit first-hand. The tour guide explained that each fruit from a cashew tree looked something like a small pear. Only one nut was produced from each fruit, growing out from the bottom of the fruit

"No wonder they are so expensive!" Simon was amazed at how long it took to collect the nuts one at a time.

Each guest sampled cashew nut juice mixed with tonic water, agreeing that it was delicious.

"That's really nice." Digby had been pleasantly surprised.

They spent an interesting hour tasting cashew products and learning about the fruit.

Some fifteen minutes later the bus came into Old Phuket town, with its pottery shops and plant nurseries on the outskirts of town. Small cottages had shrines in their front yard. Gardens bloomed with pretty flowers. Roadside stalls sold fresh fruit and vegetables.

In the town centre, markets sold both dried fish and fresh. Local restaurants provided a variety of Asian cuisines. Older buildings remained unpainted, the outside walls growing dark with mould from the moist tropical climate. Simple cottages mixed with the homes of the wealthy. On Main Street, they saw a colourful row of old shop-houses. Every kind of business seemed to be represented here. It was the kind of place that enticed the group to get out and walk around. Government buildings, museums, schools, and hospitals announced that this was the main township in Phuket. Hostels for backpackers seemed to be everywhere, Hannah noticed. She remembered how much she had enjoyed staying in hostels in her youth, but was glad to be able to afford better accommodation at this stage of her life.

From Old Phuket town, it would be possible to cross to nearby smaller islands via the road bridge to Koh Sire or the popular island-hopper ferries. The harbour was out of sight of the township and the port was still farther south on the same side of the island.

They stopped for lunch at a small family restaurant near the gardens to enjoy spring rolls and satay sticks followed by Thai green chicken curry with steamed jasmine rice.

"Yum" Jennifer confirmed.

They left with contented bellies, and Simon spoke approvingly of the local brew.

From here, the bus turned back to the lower hinterland. There was one more stop scheduled before exploring the southern beaches. Hannah had smiled when she heard Laura Glenn tell her husband how much she was looking forward to the next stop. But she had snickered when she heard Ted's groan in response.

"Bloody Hell, the battered credit card will get another whooping" Ted had complained.

14

DELIVERY

The pearl factory on Phuket Island was a popular destination, but the most popular place for the up-market traveller was the Hermann Wu Gemstone Center, which sold a variety of pearls and gems in a wondrous array of settings.

The tour guide explained, "You can take your pick from sapphires, diamonds, emeralds, topaz, or rubies as single stones. Choose a gemstone then choose your setting. Pick white gold or yellow, or even rose gold if you prefer. It will be handcrafted and delivered to you within twenty-four hours with your choice of stone. There are also over ten thousand pieces already made up for you to choose from. Earrings, necklaces, pendants for the women; cuff-links, tie tacks, and rings for the men. Then there are the objets d'art to tempt you: jewel-encrusted paperweights for your desk, statues for your living room or library."

When he got to the part about the gold-plated dinner sets and matching cutlery and hand-painted trinket jars in rich muted colors and gold decoration, Simon nudged Hannah in the ribs and whispered, "He's getting a kickback." When she shushed him, he added, "Maybe his name is U Lose."

At the Gemstone Centre, the tour guide said, "For those who do not wish to shop, there is a cafe at the rear of the store, where complimentary coffees, teas, or soft drinks are available. We will be leaving here in forty-five minutes, people."

As the group wandered into the enormous retail store, they were swarmed by the crowd of waiting sales-women who, in typical Asian fashion, accompanied them the entire time they shopped. This was a custom-ary service, yet many tourists found it overwhelming, indeed even uncomfortable and annoying.

"Have fun," Simon said as he kissed Hannah on the cheek. "Go easy on the wallet, will you please? I know you can't help yourself when it comes to buying Christmas presents for the family." He chuckled as he walked away in search of a cappuccino.

Right on cue, Hannah was joined by a petite wom-an in her forties who led her to a door on the side. Hannah sidestepped the others and disappeared through the door into the conference room.

The room was elegant, with traditional Thai stat-ues and local lacquerware souvenirs. Along one wall, a large glass cabinet was filled with Chinese jars, a nod to its owner's traditional heritage. Silk-covered settees were cosily placed around a large table with a fully stocked bar close by.

Hannah was relieved to be here and excited at the prospect of having the gemstone graded and valued. Hannah smiled to see Hermann waiting for her.

Born in 1953, Hermann Wu was the son of a Chinese importer who had begun life in Australia courtesy of his great grandparents. They had traveled there at the end of the gold-rush era, too late to make their fortunes. Hermann's father, Li, retained his Australian citizenship, though Hermann, now a resident of Vancouver, British Columbia, had chosen to apply for Canadian citizenship when he migrated as a young man. He had found that this gave him greater access to the halls of the rich around the United States, United Kingdom, and Europe.

He was well spoken, his Australian accent mingled now with a British Canadian lilt. As would be expected of one in his social class, Hermann was always elegantly groomed, though today he was a little underdressed in the heat of the tropics. His fingers were surprisingly devoid of gold or diamonds, and carried only one ring, a large milk opal—a reminder of his Australian roots.

"Welcome, my dear. It has been quite a while since we last met. I hope your family is well."

Hermann Wu had been a renowned jeweller for over thirty years. He had met Hannah at school in

Canberra, a long time ago. She had dated one of his friends, though she was some years his junior. Their paths had crossed again back in 2003 when she was in Canada on another sojourn. The experience had proven fortuitous for both. On that occasion, Hannah had walked away with just over three million dollars. Hermann had taken a similar share, and both were now quiet owners of Swiss bank accounts as a result. It was Hermann who had initiated the project, though Hannah was the one to retrieve the stones.

Hermann's specialty was diamonds and he was known for only dealing in gemstones of at least five carats. Otherwise, they were just not worth his while. In fact, he had recently sold a diamond so large that the ring setting had to be carried across not one, but two fingers on its owner's hand. There was still plenty of money in New York, Hollywood, Florida, and London! Most gemstones of this size were reserved for special customers ready to pay handsomely for a new trinket.

Diamonds, Hermann had explained to Hannah when they first started working together, come in many colours: blue like the Hope Diamond, pink like the Williamson Pink that had been given to Queen Elizabeth II on her wedding day in 1947, yellow like the Florentine Diamond now lost to the world. There were also clear, of course, as well as red and brown. The most unusual of all, the Koi Diamond, had the unique coloring of koi fish, graduating from white, orange, light yellow, dark blue, and black. Hermann dreamed of holding the Koi Diamond one day.

Hannah remembered Hermann explaining, "Diamonds can be easily overlooked in their natural state if you don't know what to look for. Imagine a lump of washing soda in the rough. Really, it's quite unremarkable when found, usually in alluvial deposits. You would almost ignore it with its outer surface looking battered and dull. In fact, if they have the usual opaque skin on them, diamonds look almost like gum."

Diamonds had fascinated Hermann from an early age, when he stumbled across one with his grandfather while on vacation in the Kimberley region of Western Australia. He wished he had found more, but that small twenty-five-point diamond was enough to capture his imagination for bigger and better things. Grandad Li Qiang, known as "King," had taken him to sift sediment in the King George River because Grandad thought the name of the river was a good omen.

King had found several small diamonds that day, back in September 1966, in a region where others were later found by geologists. Hermann laughed as he said, "If King had used his tobacco habit as an omen and moved farther south to Smoke Creek, he could have been the one to find fifteen diamonds in his sifting pan. Instead it was the geologists from the Argyle

Mines exploration team who found them less than
a decade later. The rest, as they say, is history. More
than eight hundred million carats of diamonds have
come from what is now known as the world's largest
diamond supplier, particularly pink diamonds that are
practically synonymous with the Argyle Mine."

Hermann wasn't fussy about a diamond's colour;
he could find buyers for any of them. His reputation in
the world of the uber-rich was well known.

"I was pleasantly surprised to get your message
and, of course, only too happy to see you again,"
he said to Hannah. "I met with the Frenchman this
morning and have his deposit with me already. We
will gather the remaining gold in the next few days
as agreed. I have not asked where the gold came
from. I thought you might like to tell me." Hermann
waited, but Hannah just smiled her most mysterious
smile.

"You have piqued my curiosity, Hannah. Tell me
what you have to show me today." Hermann wondered
what would entice Hannah to this part of the world.
He could not imagine what she would have to share
with him from this region, as it was not known for diamonds. Surely he would already know about anything
special that might become available.

"Well, you can take a look at these smaller stones
later," said Hannah as she emptied a bag of emeralds,
rubies, amethysts, and smaller diamonds onto the desk
in front of her.

Even Hermann, used to handling all kinds of gems on a regular basis, seemed surprised at the quality and quantity in front of him. "These are the small ones?" he asked.

"Ever heard of the Shwedagon Diamond?" She chuckled with glee.

"Indeed I have," Hermann said, looking slightly perplexed. "Said to be around seventy-six carats and believed to have been brought to Burma from the Indian diamond mines."

"Well, I hope you have a buyer for it, Hermann, because it was quite an adventure to get hold of it," Hannah said.

"You best show it to me, Hannah, I am waiting with bated breath." Hermann stretched out his palm to receive the prize. "If this is what you say it is, then I am very much looking forward to holding it. But how did you manage to come by it?"

Hannah handed over the box with an enormous sense of pride. "Believe me, you don't want to know. But it's hard to believe no one else has ever coveted this gemstone enough to go after it."

"I heard there was an earthquake," Hermann persisted. "Did you pull it out of the rubble?"

"Not exactly." She gave him a smug look, which he returned with a blank expression.

"If this is the Shwedagon, then I would estimate its value somewhere between twenty-three and thirty-three million dollars, depending on its cut and quality, though I suspect it would have to be recut into small-er stones. You may know that the Archduke Joseph diamond, also a colourless seventy-six-carat Indian diamond, sold at Christies in 2012 for twenty-one-point-four million dollars." Hermann rattled on as he picked up the stone.

He turned the stone over in his hands, savouring the moment, and then lifted it to the light to check its refractivity. Diamonds have a strikingly brilliant appearance as the light that passes through them is bent sharply. Hermann knew that a real diamond will have a significant sparkle, not to be confused with re-flections, which would be the next thing he checked for.

"Reflections" referred to the colour of the refract-ed light, which should be intense. If these were gray shades, authenticity was more likely; whereas rainbow reflections tended to indicate either a fake or a poor quality diamond. Hermann looked straight down through the top of the diamond to confirm its quality. He then tried the newspaper test, to see if he could "read" through the diamond.

Hermann pulled a powerful microscope from its case and lifted it onto the table. Hannah can't resist this kind of tech, and notices that it has a 1200x pow-er scope. He drew out sturdy tweezers to pick up the large stone and manoeuver it with the top facet down, placing the stone under the scope. He began rocking the gem back and forth, checking for any flash that showed a slight orange along the facets, which could indicate a man-made stone. He emitted a "hmm," and Hannah frowned.

Hermann picked up a pen light and, holding the stone close to his eye, shone the light through the stone. He was checking for rainbow colours made by a double refraction, which would indicate the presence of moissanite, once found in meteors but today only found in laboratories.

Hermann raised his jeweler's loupe to his eye. The glass allowed him to see the characteristics that would enable a grading: he must look for "inclusions," small mineral flecks and slight changes in colour only visible through the lens.

As Hannah knew well by this time, a jeweller must assess colour, cut, clarity, and carat size; this takes a little time but needs careful consideration. Hermann's hands were steady and his face expressionless as he went through the techniques of his trade.

He returned the loupe to the desk and produced his jewellers' scales, placing them on the table between himself and Hannah, with the dial facing him. Hannah understood that this very precise tool would enable him to get an accurate assessment of carat size. Diamonds were around 0.2 grams per carat, whereas cubic zirconia, for example, were about 50 percent heavier than that.

He frowned. "Weight of this one is just over twenty-two grams — larger than the Akbar Shah, also a colourless diamond out of India. Sadly, its whereabouts are unknown since it was recut to seventy-one-point-two carats in the 1880s. It was originally part of the Peacock Throne, you know, with various inscriptions from AD 1039, but its new owner, one George Blogg, had them removed when he had it recut." Hermann was certainly talkative.

"George Blogg?" Hannah asked, smiling.

"Yes," said Hermann, "that really was his name."

Hermann continued his examination. "Hmm, let me say, the cut on this one would be graded not as an ideal but certainly as an excellent. Clarity grade is definitely an FL and the color is a D, a clear colourless stone." Hermann continued. "The shape is an ancient point cut, deep set, typical of the thirteenth century. Polishing of the octahedral face creates even facets, unblemished from what was probably an otherwise un-appealing rough. The cut definitely dates it from the mid-fourteenth century. Both the pavilion and crown have open pointed tables that make the true colour more visible to the eye. It also shows up any cut flaws, and this one has none."

Hannah smiled shamelessly at this, knowing it would improve both the ease of selling and the price of the stone.

As he held the gem in his hands, Hermann brought it close to his mouth and breathed on it repeatedly.

"What on earth are you doing now, Hermann?" Hannah asked. "It looks most unscientific."

"Patience, please, dear." Hermann had now gone through all the rituals of testing available to him. He resorted to puffing at the stone, knowing that the fog test could show a fake. Real diamonds dispersed heat from the breath instantly, whereas fakes took longer to clear.

"Would you mind turning out the lights, please, Hannah? Yes, that switch near the door please, dear."

Now Hannah was really perplexed. She had never seen Hermann conduct such thorough testing. Crossing the room to the light switch, she was growing anxious.

With the room now in darkness, Hermann flicked on the ultraviolet light he carried with him. Most diamonds will show a blue fluorescence when exposed to ultraviolet or black light. Hermann was looking for a medium to strong blue to confirm the diamond's authenticity. If a blue fluorescence were absent, the stone might be a fake. But some real diamonds did not fluoresce under ultraviolet light, either. A yellowy-green or even gray fluorescence under the light could indicate moissanite. While this test was not conclusive in itself—some fake diamonds had been known to be treated to fluoresce under a UV light. At best, this was just another indicator.

He put down the light, and Hannah turned the room lights back on. Hermann drew a deep breath before continuing — what he was about to say would not be well received.

"There is a problem," Hermann said quietly.

"Excuse me," Hannah almost stuttered. "What did you say? What is it — poor quality?"

"Hannah, bear with me please while I explain." Hermann looked nervous. "This one is interesting because it is the first time a culet has been seen in a point-cut diamond. They would have to have been well ahead of themselves on shape design to include a culet, because these were not seen elsewhere around the world until the table cut was introduced.

"Let me explain. A culet was a flat-face cut at the bottom of the gemstone. The word derives from the Latin *culus*, meaning bottom. Now, on a diamond where cleavage planes run parallel to the octahedral face, a split in the diamond could occur up the entire length of the pavilion if the tip at the base is left as a point cut. The culet protects the integrity of the stone by protecting its fragile tip. When the table cut was introduced, the culet mirrored the table at the top. So the cut is out of character with the era.

"It is also too heavy to be a real diamond. It should be around fifteen grams, but this is nearly half that again, which says cubic zirconia to me. I am sorry, Hannah, but this is a synthetic diamond. A gem this perfect is usually a fake. A cubic zirconia will pass most tests, and usually they don't have imperfections because they come from a sterile lab. I can therefore tell you that, without a shadow of a doubt, this is a really good copy but definitely not the genuine article."

"Bullshit!" Hannah blurted. Her face paled to a deathly white as she struggled to understand what Hermann had just told her. She steadied herself against a side table but could feel her legs giving way beneath her. She started to tremble. "Not possible," she whimpered.

15

SCAM

"Well," said Hermann, "I was suspicious as soon as you said it was the Shwedagon, because I had heard stories about them hiding the genuine article."

"But how?"

"Here, let me get you a chair—and some brandy, by the looks of it." He crossed the room to the bar, grabbed a large crystal balloon glass, and poured a generous slurp of brandy into it. Passing the glass to Hannah, he began to explain what he knew of the Shwedagon Diamond.

"There were stories circulating in the war years about the Japanese when they finished the Burma Railway, or the Death Railway as it was known. Do you know, of the nearly two hundred thousand forced labourers from Asia and the sixty thousand POWs, some ninety thousand died — one in three

— horrific statistics. Anyway, I digress; the stories were that the Japanese had plotted to steal the Shwedagon Diamond.

"The story goes that the Japanese lost face after originally promising to grant Burma Independence, and then reneging on that promise and declaring Burma a fully sovereign state of Japan in 1943 under Colonel Suzuki. Burma's General Aung San had called for the Burmese to co-operate with the British and, indeed, even the Russians, behind Suzuki's back. When Suzuki found out that the Burmese army was preparing a rebellion, he turned his back on them, and it's believed that Colonel Suzuki was determined to teach them a lesson.

"His private complaints to the Japanese army colonels in Burma with him at the time, resulted in a plot to shame the Burmese. The story goes that they plotted a raid on the Shwedagon Pagoda to steal the diamond. Remember, this was seen as the most important religious and cultural structure in all of Burma. Clearly the Japanese soldiers, who were in Rangoon at the time, had no regard for karma when it came to the diamond!

"Well, Buddhists are pacifists but they are not stupid. When they heard of the Japanese plot to deprive them of their sacred diamond, a dozen monks who were trustees of the stupa, formed a plan to protect the diamond forever. Under cover of darkness, they scaled the spire, removing their diamond. The Japanese could not steal it because it was not there when they tried to take it."

"So where is it?" Hannah asked.

"Rumour has it that it's hidden deep within the pagoda." Hermann said. "Legend states that among the Buddhist relics in the centre of the stupa are even more riches, unimaginable riches, buried in a square chamber that is filled with layers of jewels. No one but the monks know where it is, and no one but them can access it. While this has never been proven one way or the other, it certainly adds to the mystery. Folklore has it that this is where the real Shwedagon Diamond now resides. In other words, they hid it in their own ancient safe!"

"Bloody hell!" Hannah interjected.

"And, I'm sorry to say," resumed Hermann, "inspecting this today just re-affirms that the Buddhist trustees did in fact remove the original and later replaced it with a simulated diamond. Anyway, back to the war years. The Burmese, along with the Brits, chased the Japanese out of town, so that was the end of the Japanese occupation of Burma. But I often wonder if Suzuki got away with other gems? Was that the beginnings of the Suzuki Motor Company, do you think?" Hermann laughed. "Just joking!"

Hannah didn't laugh. She felt nauseated. "So," she asked quietly, "why didn't the Japanese take the whole orb?"

"Because, dear girl, it was simply too heavy." Hermann chuckled. "There are over eighteen hundred carats of diamonds on the orb, plus the gold, which makes it much too heavy to remove easily. It would take days to erect scaffolding to even approach the orb. Hardly something the Japanese could do undisturbed and undiscovered! Even the vane weighs more than four hundred kilos. Anyway, the top of the orb was without a central diamond for many years. It was only after the earthquake of 1970 knocked the whole shaft of the crown umbrella out of alignment that scaffolding was erected and extensive repairs were undertaken. This is when the trustees had a fake diamond crafted and had it placed back into the orb at the top of Shwedagon. It has to be, because they couldn't have had a cubic zirconium replica created before that decade. Though I suppose they could have had a glass replica there until then. Anyway, there it has sat ever since."

"Why replace it with a fake?" asked Hannah, still shaking her head.

"Well, the trustees wanted to ensure the Burmese people still believed the diamond was there, and to ensure the original design of the structure was held inviolate for future generations."

"Ha," said Hannah. "In other words they were scammed?"

"Let's just call it a good marketing ploy," Hermann said, with a deprecating laugh. "There were a very select few who knew anything about it."

"So how did they keep it a secret all these years?" Hannah was numb.

"You have to understand," continued Hermann, "that two hundred fifty thousand Burmese died under Japanese rule, and even when the Japanese surrendered to the Allies, Burma was left under a military administration. People were scared. There were even calls for Aung San to be tried for his involvement in a murder during military operations in 1942. He was well liked by his countrymen, but that did not stop him from being assassinated in 1947."

"How do you know the story so well?" Hannah asked.

Hermann explained, "My uncle worked on the railway during the war. He fell in love with a Burmese girl, married her, and stayed on in Burma. He later became one of the Shwedagon trustees in the decades after the war. In fact he and Aunty still live in Yangon."

Hannah dropped her head forward to hide her shame at missing the main prize.

"I'm sorry Hannah, had I known you were interested in it, I could have told you this before. Let's assume that you have at least escaped the bad karma associated with owning such a diamond, a bit like the Hope Diamond's reputation for tragedy befalling those who owned it." Hermann paused. "I guess you weren't meant to have it. Call it karma."

"Then karma sucks!" snorted Hannah. She started to walk away in disgust, wondering how she would explain this to the team she had enlisted to help with the project. "See what you can do with the other stones then, and just send my money to the usual account please. At least you'll get market value for the gold."

"Of course, my dear," he said, watching her closely. Hermann picked up the box the gem had arrived in and attempted to return it to Hannah.

"Look, I need to do more testing on it because it may be moissanite, not cubic zirconia. Either way, it has some value, Hannah, but certainly not the millions you were hoping for. Do you still want me to manage it?"

"All right, Hermann, just get me what you can for it!"

Herman watched her departure, closed the door behind her, and walked back to the desk. He re-adjusted the scales back to zero from the seven grams showing on the display, and smiled to himself.

"Amazing what a little research and a little story-telling can achieve. Karma works for some," he chuckles to himself.

"Having a silent partner hasn't hurt!" Jean-Pierre sneered as he stepped from the shadows.

"Absolutely!" replied Hermann. "You are my best business partner to date, Jean-Pierre. And let me tell you, this is one truly remarkable diamond."

Hermann collected the Shwedagon Diamond and put it in his glasses case in his shirt pocket. Thankfully, diamonds did not show up in metal detectors, so it would easily go undetected at the airport. No Customs official would know he was carrying the best part of thirty million dollars in his pocket. He regularly carried diamonds from one country to another this way.

Smiling at Jean-Pierre, Hermann patted his pocket and started calling his contact list. The smaller stones could be dealt with by his staff here in Phuket, and the gold put to use in his jewellery stores across Thailand and Malaysia.

16

AMSTERDAM

Hermann spent a week in Kuala Lumpur doing the deal on the Shwedagon Diamond. In the end, it was something of an auction between three main bidders. Money always won; there were no favourites when it came to fortunes made and lost. The new owner, a media mogul in China, had a lot of money to spend on trinkets. He even topped an Arabian oil magnate and a Russian businessman. That was no small feat.

Agreeing on a base price for the gemstone, Hermann then set about designing a setting for the main stone. The buyer wanted one large stone set, and an array of smaller stones to put aside for investment. This would give him the best value for his purchase while hiding the origin of the large stone.

A very substantial deposit was paid to Hermann via bank draft. It was equivalent to half the final amount of the deal that had been struck. Hermann was fourteen million dollars better off, with the same amount due on completion. With a few small costs incurred along the way, including half a million paid to Hannah, he was still left with a vast profit.

He would take care of Jean-Pierre at a later date. Hermann had decided he would simply pay him a small amount and not tell him the actual value of the deal that was done. He could convince Jean-Pierre that it had proved an almost impossible stone to move in the underground market. Let's face it; this diamond was not going to public auction, so who would know the true value of the deal that was done. He could pay Jean-Pierre a couple of million and leave it at that. Without prior knowledge of the escapade, the scam would not have been possible. Hermann owed the Frenchman.

The other gemstones sold for two point three million dollars, and the gold was sold at market value. Some gold was absorbed into Hermann's businesses across Asia, and Hannah was paid her fair share for all of these. It did not make sense for Hermann to push the envelope too far. After all, Hannah was a good investment for future deals, even if he had double-crossed her on this one. She had still made a handsome profit on her adventure. Hermann knew he could only ever double-cross her once.

With Christmas and New Year now upon him, the world seemed to come to a halt while holidays were taken in almost every country. A side trip to Beijing to meet with the buyer gave Hermann his instructions on the design of the finished piece. They poured over drawings for several hours a day over three days, until the buyer was happy with Hermann's design.

Hermann returned to his showroom in Kuala Lumpur to refine the drawings and contact the diamond cutter. Having found a buyer for the Shwedagon Diamond, Hermann now had to arrange for the diamond to be precision cut. It was late January before he was ready to move the diamond to the cutting room.

He needed an expert eye to cut such an immense stone, and there were only two places in the world capable of handling this assignment with expertise and discretion.

While Bruges in Belgium is often described as the world's centre for diamonds, Hermann's preference was for Amsterdam. His contacts there were always discrete and he did not mind paying handsomely for that discretion.

He booked a business-class flight from Kuala Lumpur to Amsterdam at an exorbitant price. Booking flights at short notice meant paying a premium.

Hermann would travel to Amsterdam, meet with the diamond cutter, leave the stone for cutting, and head home to Canada. It was a fairly short flight back from Canada to collect the diamonds when they were ready. He could return to Malaysia to set the largest stone, and then fly on to Beijing to deliver it within a few days.

Malaysian Airlines' Flight 16 was due to depart Kuala Lumpur just before midnight, so Hermann made the most of a late dinner in town before heading for the airport. The taxi dropped him at the terminal at Kuala Lumpur International airport just before ten o'clock.

At least flying business class meant that check-in was relatively quick and painless. He was thankful that he had not been directed to the body scanner as he passed through Customs and Immigration.

Like most businessmen, Hermann travelled only with carry-on luggage whenever possible. While it saved time at the baggage carousel on arrival, it also meant he had to drag it around the airport with him. This was much less of a nuisance now that luggage had wheels. Travelling the world might seem glamorous, but it is surprising how much time a person must spend sitting around airports waiting for flights. One can only spend so much time working on e-mails before getting bored. Hermann spent a lot of time in business-class lounges in airports all around the world. They had become like second offices to him over the years. He produced his boarding pass at the door to the lounge and was quickly admitted.

He settled in with his usual glass of Johnnie Walker Black on ice. He liked a scotch because it helped him

sleep during the flight. It worked better than a sleeping pill and tasted a whole lot better, too.

The plane, scheduled for midnight, departed only
six minutes late. By twelve thirty, Hermann was asleep
in his flatbed — the most expensive night's accommodation he had ever paid for.

He was woken by the flight attendant just before
5:15 a.m., Amsterdam time. This gave him time for
breakfast and a quick change of clothes before the seat-
belt light came on for the approach to Amsterdam's
Schiphol airport for landing.

By the time he had deplaned and passed through
Immigration and Customs, it was nearly 7:45 a.m.
Hermann checked his luggage in at the storage counter for collection later in the day. This morning he had
time to kill, so he opted for the train into town rather
than a taxi. He made the long walk down to the train
station underneath Schiphol airport for a train into
Amsterdam city. Hermann had to purchase a ticket at
the service counter, having no local currency for the
ticketing machines.

The board directed him to the platform for the
next train into town. He had a ten-minute wait. He rode
the escalator down one floor to the station platform.
The train arrived precisely on time, as was the way in
the Netherlands. Everything ran on time. Hermann
stepped into a clean carriage, and took an empty seat.
Around him students had their heads down, staring at
laptops, plugged in to the onboard Wi-Fi. He always

found trains in Europe to be very civilised and commuter friendly.

It was an easy journey into town. By eight thirty, Hermann was exiting the Amsterdam Central Station. He walked outside onto Stationsplein. His appointment was not until eleven, so he decided to take a walk to clear his head of jet lag.

Leaving the train station, Hermann was always amused that the first thing you saw was the parking station for all the bicycles used by the locals. With over a million bicycles in Amsterdam, bicycle parking became a critical element of daily life. Amsterdam was one of the most bike-friendly capitals in the world, but it was the only one he knew of with an actual parking station for bikes at the central train station.

Hermann was careful walking down the street, though. While bikes had the right of way and their own traffic lane, it was still too easy to step off the footpath into the path of a bike rider. A friend had actually been charged and fined for knocking a rider off his bike, as bikes had precedence on the roads. That friend had been left with a bruised shoulder, a bruised ego, and a bruised wallet.

Hermann always found that Amsterdam, capital of the Kingdom of the Netherlands, was one of the world's most beautiful cities, with its unique architecture and numerous canals. It was a city where walking was easy and enjoyable.

Its name derived from the dam on the river Amstel. Originally a small fishing village, Amsterdam became an important port for sea trade during the seventeenth century. The city was renowned as the centre of finance and diamonds during that era. The influence of the Dutch was felt worldwide. Ships sailed from Amsterdam across the world to North America, Africa, Indonesia, India, and Sri Lanka, as well as the Baltic and Brazil. The Dutch East India Company prospered and became famous for trading its own shares on what became the world's first stock exchange.

Hermann turned onto Prins Hendrikkade heading for the borough of Jordaan. Thankful for his winter coat against the crisp morning air, he had pulled on his gloves and scarf, and donned a cap. He had done this walk many times before, and it always felt like coming home. He loved the markets and boutique artisan stores. He had an eye for the finer things in life, so he appreciated the work on display here. There was little open at this hour, but the window shopping made it all worthwhile. He watched families appear from the tall houses, pushing onto bikes for the ride to work or school.

He followed Prins Hendrikkade until he came in sight of Ronde Lutherse Kerk, and then crossed the bridge heading for Prinsengrachte canal, down past Anne Frank's house to Westermarkt.

The architecture and colours of the buildings brought the streets alive. It was a joy to wander through these boroughs, even with snow on the ground. Some of the world's narrowest houses were in Amsterdam. Land tax was applied on the width of the land, so the smart locals built only narrow houses that were very tall, some up to four stories high. The world's narrowest house was here in Amsterdam — only the width of a double bed but several stories tall.

Hermann ventured on through the Negen Straatjes area (meaning Nine Little Streets), and then cut across to the Bloemenmarkt to marvel at the tulip bulbs.

The variety of tulips available was staggering. While none were in bloom in late January, the bulbs were still available. Some were as big as a human head and others simply tiny. The array of colours that could normally be seen here always staggered Hermann, and he was tempted to make a side trip to the tulip auctions just out of town, where thousands of flowers would be trucked in from hot houses to supply the worlds thirst for tulips. The markets themselves were vast, the size of several football fields.

The little stores along this part of the canal were still selling leftover Christmas decorations. Traditional Delft blue had been styled into miniature houses and other trinkets, including ornaments representing pottery teddy bears and the inevitable "boy and girl" style, which were also popular as salt-and-pepper shakers. Hermann wondered how many tourists went home with these classic mementos of a trip to Holland every year.

Hermann realized he had walked for over an hour and a half and was suddenly tired. He spent a quiet half hour at a corner café, recharging his batteries with coffee and a pastry. Exiting the café, he hailed a taxi to take him the short distance to Nieuwe Uilenburgerstraat for his eleven o'clock meeting.

Amsterdam had been a diamond centre for centuries. Sephardic Jews started a diamond-cutting industry in the sixteenth century, with the diamond market being established there in the nineteenth. At the many diamond companies around town, there were private rooms available for commercial jewellers from all over the world.

Discretion was assured. The Diamond Museum housed replicas of the British crown jewels and the Dutch coronation gems. A local diamond factory, Coster, had been asked to polish the Koh-i-Noor diamond for Queen Victoria of England. These businesses were well respected. Amsterdam was a centre of excellence.

Security was always tight at these places — understandable, given the millions of dollars of gemstones kept on hand. Tourists could visit by invitation, and busloads arrived daily for free tours. Guides escorted visitors through security and into the showrooms. They were happy to explain the history of diamond cutting and the settings they worked on daily for clients around the world. Sometimes a visitor might even get to handle the diamonds as well, but under very strict conditions and with a multitude of recording devices trained on the process all the time.

Hermann greeted the receptionist at Diamond House and said, "Hermann Wu for an eleven o'clock meeting with Caspar Smit, please."

"Please take a seat, Mr. Wu, and I will let Mr. Smit know you have arrived."

Hermann had been a regular visitor here for years and knew it would only take a few minutes before he was escorted up to meet Caspar. Hermann believed names were often appropriate to the destiny of their owner. This was confirmed when he found out that the name Caspar meant "treasure hunter'"—an appropriate name for someone working with diamonds.

"Please follow me, Mr. Wu," Caspar's assistant hailed him from the doorway. She ushered him into the antiquated elevator and pushed the button for level two.

Caspar Smit rose from his desk as Hermann was ushered into his office.

"Hermann, so good of you to honour us with a visit today," said Caspar. "I hope the holiday season has not caused you too much delay."

"Not at all," Hermann lied. "Did you enjoy a pleasant break over Christmas?"

"Indeed, thank you for asking." The small talk continued for some minutes while they caught up with talk of holidays, family news, and current affairs.

Eventually Hermann withdrew the Shwedagon Diamond from his coat pocket. "This one is special, Caspar."

"My oh my." Caspar sighed at the first glimpse of such an enormous diamond. "Show me your designs for this beauty. Are we keeping it as one stone?"

There would be no questions as to the origin of the diamond, and provenance and ownership were always assumed with customers as well known as Hermann Wu.

"Not this time," Hermann said. He pulled the design work from his inside coat pocket. The two men huddled over the design for more than an hour, in deep discussion over cutting, facets, and design detail.

Caspar finally lifted his head from the drawings and consulted his schedule. "Of course this can be achieved, Hermann, but there will be a couple of weeks' delay. It is quite intricate, and I am booked up for the next month. Does that still work for you?"

"That's fine,'" replied Hermann. "You are the man for the job, so we will wait until you can fit it in to your schedule. It has to be your work, though, not a junior cutter."

"Yes, I understand," Caspar agreed. "It will really be something special when it is cut and set. I will be honoured to work on it for you." He made some calculations on the notepad in front of him and tickled the calculator next to him. Caspar then wrote out a formal quote for the work to be done and handed the work order to Hermann for his signature. Once signed, this would constitute agreement to pay for the work or surrender the gem to the cutting house.

"Just the cutting please, Caspar. We will see to the setting ourselves." Hermann often divided the work this way. He took great pride in putting his artistic talents to work to refine the finished piece. That was how he had earned his reputation as one of the world's best jewellers.

"That's not a problem," said Caspar, pushing the quote across the desk for Hermann to see. "If you will just sign the work order and agree to the quote, we can get the job scheduled for you."

Hermann signed the bottom of the quote, noting how prices had risen since his last visit, and then returned the document to Caspar.

"I will let you know when the cutting and polishing are complete." Caspar added the job to his diary and logged it into the operations schedule on the company's secure computer. "It will be slow going, so I have added some leeway to the schedule to be sure. I assume somewhere around the first week in March, at this stage."

Hermann nodded his assent, rose from the chair, and bade Caspar farewell. A slight woman appeared at the doorway to escort Hermann back to reception.

A taxi arrived promptly to take him to his next destination. There was a memorable address in the Red Light District that would give him an hour's welcome relief. Then he would enjoy a really good steak at a favourite little restaurant off NieuwMarkt.

After that he would return to Schiphol, collect his luggage, and transfer to the Sheraton Airport Hotel for his flight home in the morning via London to Vancouver.

Now the wait began.

17

HERMANN

Hermann was in New York when the call came from Caspar.

"Hermann, the work is complete a little earlier than I had expected. I must say I think the finished stone is incredible. It's not often I get excited about a finished cut," Caspar said with enthusiasm. "You were right to go for the added facets. Our new cutting technique makes this look fantastic with one hundred twenty-one facets. You must promise to send me a photo of the finished piece for my album."

"Thanks, Caspar. I'll collect the stones on Monday." Hermann was looking forward to seeing the finished piece. "I assume the smaller stones are also ready?"

"Yes, of course," Caspar confirmed. "Monday works fine for me. See you then."

Well, there go tonight's theatre tickets, Hermann mused.

Hermann called his executive assistant and asked her to clear his calendar for the coming week. This was the biggest payday he had seen for some time, so everything else was secondary.

He had assistants to take over when these things pulled him away from his scheduled commitments. Customers would understand, even if it meant giving them something for nothing — or perhaps just a discount, if they complained. He could always feign illness if nothing else worked.

A phone call to Beijing at this hour would be inappropriate if it drew his customer from slumber. It was ten thirty on a cold New York morning, which meant almost midnight in China. He would wait until he landed in Amsterdam to call his client to give him a progress report.

Hermann e-mailed his showroom in Kuala Lumpur and asked for his private facilities to be prepared for his arrival Tuesday. He would be exhausted, but he could sleep on the plane. That was the whole reason for paying for business class.

He wanted to be in his own showroom in Kuala Lumpur to manage the setting of the larger stone himself. This was what he had promised his Beijing buyer. His team would ensure everything was ready for him. He had two assistants standing by to help craft the gold setting, ready to take the cut stone.

An hour later, his executive assistant called him with details of his flight from New York back to

Amsterdam and then on to Kuala Lumpur. She would advise his housekeeper of his pending arrival in Kuala Lumpur. Nothing would be overlooked.

Hermann still had time for a decent lunch in New York and managed to change his theatre tickets to the matinee performance. This was a move that satisfied his companion and got Hermann off the hook for flying out at short notice.

Yet another taxi and another boarding pass brought Hermann to New York's John F. Kennedy International Airport. Named in memory of a much loved US president shot down in Dallas, Texas, some fifty years earlier, JFK was a very busy airport. The taxi delivered him to Terminal One for check-in.

Security at US borders had become an horrific experience since 9/11. Hermann would have to allow at least an extra hour. Progress here was slow and painful. Staff members were trained not to be friendly, and their training showed. *Remove your shoes, remove your belt, and hope your trousers don't fall down,* he thought. *Place your wallet, your phone, your keys, and your change into the black tray for x-ray. You even have to take your hat off.* He knew the routine off by heart.

KLM shared a business-class lounge with Air France at JFK. After check-in, Hermann made his way there, entering the door near Gate One.

His flight would depart New York's JFK airport at 6:50 p.m. and was due to arrive into Amsterdam at 7:05 a.m. local time on Monday. There was an earlier flight that got in at some ungodly hour. However, there was no point in the earlier flight, as he would not be able to go directly to the Diamond House.

Caspar had agreed to an early meeting and would be there at 8:30 a.m. A limousine had been booked to meet Hermann's flight and take him directly to his meeting with Caspar. That would give him an hour and a half to inspect the stones and then return by limo to the airport. There was a flight at noon to Kuala Lumpur. This was cutting it close, but if he needed more time with Caspar, his executive assistant would reschedule him onto the evening flight instead.

His flight was called on time and departed as planned, despite the drifting snow that had started to fall late in the New York winter. Hermann enjoyed another scotch and a delicious three-course dinner. Flying business class meant several finer points to the trip, one of which was the meal served on beautiful crockery and with top wine selections. Hermann changed into airline pyjamas supplied to each business-class guest.

He appreciated the fully flat seat, especially its length and privacy canopy. He settled in with his personal entertainment system's large screen, selecting a new-release movie. The flight attendants had delivered his comfort kit and his Delft blue miniature house filled with Dutch gin. Sleep would not be far away, even though his body clock would still complain tomorrow.

The Boeing 777 landed at Schiphol airport fifteen minutes early, and the lines at Immigration were short. Hermann was concerned that the chauffeur would not be there when he made it through the Customs Hall.

He was proved wrong when he saw a tall, slender blonde man in uniform with a sign showing Hermann's name. He identified himself and was led to the waiting vehicle.

Traffic was starting to build at the approaching morning peak hour as workers headed into the city. It was five minutes to eight when the limo pulled up to the gate at the Diamond House. Hermann took the driver's business card and promised to call him when the meeting finished. At the latest, the limo was to be back here by ten o'clock for the return trip to Schiphol.

He hoped someone was here early, as he did not fancy standing in the cold waiting for Caspar. He had called the diamond cutter when he landed, so Caspar knew he was ahead of schedule. Hermann approached the closed gate and pushed the intercom button to speak to security.

"Goedemorgen," a deep voice boomed from the intercom.

"Hermann Wu for Caspar Smit, please?" Hermann announced.

"Thank you, Mr. Wu. Please enter through the small gate to your left. Our staff will greet you momentarily to escort you to Mr. Smit." The voice now sounded a little friendlier and spoke in English.

A matronly woman in security garb arrived almost instantly, greeting Hermann and leading him through the parking lot toward the building. There was little conversation until the elevator arrived, and Hermann was told, "Mr. Smit will meet you on Level Two."

Sure enough, as the elevator doors opened, there stood Caspar.

"My friend, welcome back!" Caspar greeted him.

"Please accept my thanks for seeing me so early. One can never tell with airline schedules," Hermann apologized.

"Not at all. These things happen." Caspar was very accommodating. "I am pleased to be able to deliver these to you in person." Caspar crossed the room and dialled a code into the wall safe. When the outer door opened, he then placed his thumb against the inner keypad, to gain access to the high-tech safe.

"Did you have any problems?" Hermann asked.

"Not really, though a lot of time and precision had to be employed. We wanted to get the right cuts to maximise the yield from such a large stone." Caspar was clearly proud of his achievements with this job. He turned and walked back to the showroom table where a cloth lay unfurled before him, ready to accept the contents of the tray marked "Wu."

Caspar continued. "The main stone, as you know, was the challenge. I hope you agree it is stupendous!" He placed the tray alongside the jewellery roll and slid the lid back to reveal a large, sparkling stone embraced by several smaller diamonds.

Hermann's eyes widened at the sight before him. For a man who had spent many years with gems of all sizes and values, he was almost speechless. "Magnificent." Hermann finally exhaled. He picked up the tweezers and lifted the stone from its shrine.

The men spent two hours inspecting and cataloguing each of the stones — fifteen in all. The company cashier arrived and took payment for the work, which was then processed through the banking networks and transferred into the account of the Diamond House. This would have to be completed before the stones could be signed back over to Hermann.

He thanked Caspar before taking his leave and being escorted back to the front gate. Security did not leave his side until he stepped into the limousine and left the company premises.

The limousine had been hired through a special security company that screened all drivers. They were well paid for transporting these clients from the Diamond House to the airport. It was astonishing how many diamonds left the country each year.

Insurance was usually taken out on diamond consignments moving around the world. However, no insurance policy could ever replace the stones Hermann had with him now. These were priceless and stolen, so he had foregone insurance on this shipment. It would have been too difficult to forge the paperwork necessary to satisfy the insurance company of the origin and ownership of the Shwedagon Diamond. He did not want to complicate the process.

Hermann had made these trips hundreds of times in the last thirty years without incident. It was not uncommon for him to have the gemstone set by the cutter. Hermann would then wear the piece to the airport.

Occasionally he would take a female assistant with him. It went unnoticed when a well-dressed, attractive woman arrived home wearing glamorous jewellery. He had brought millions of dollars of gems into many countries without declaring them. It saved a lot of money on customs duties and import taxes.

Today, the stones travelled in his inside pocket, especially zippered, ready for this precious cargo. He kept patting his pocket unconsciously. If anyone was watching him, they would have recognised the gesture as protecting something of value.

Traffic was now slightly heavier than on the trip into town, and time was not on his side. Check-in opened at 10:00 a.m. for the noon flight. It was now 10:15 a.m., and they were still some way from Schiphol.

He had to check in before eleven to be at the gate by eleven thirty. This was going to be tight, even with priority gates through security for business-class passengers.

The limo pulled up at 11:02 a.m. Hermann thanked the driver, grabbed his flight bag, and scurried away to the KLM counter. He glanced at the destination board and sighed with relief when he saw "Delayed" against his KLM flight to Kuala Lumpur.

The flight from Amsterdam back to Kuala Lumpur was KLM4123, a code-share flight operated by Malaysian Airlines as their Flight 19. It had suffered a small technical issue prior to departing Kuala Lumpur, so it was an hour and a half late arriving into Amsterdam.

Hermann checked in, passed quickly through security and Immigration and headed straight for the business-class lounge. He made a beeline to the free bar, poured himself a glass of the Haig that was on offer, and dropped into a nearby comfy chair.

His body clock was shot; it was still early morning in New York, where he had spent the last week. It was hard to justify the scotch, but he needed it right now. It barely touched the sides.

Refilling his glass with Haig and ice, he set it down alongside his chair and wandered off to find some lunch. At least he could do the right thing by his stomach if he was drinking at what felt like breakfast time.

Instead of arriving in Kuala Lumpur at seven on Tuesday morning, the delayed flight touched down at 8:20 a.m. Hermann's driver met him, taking his flight bag from him. The driver ushered him to the waiting vehicle, opened the back door, closed it gently after

Hermann entered, and then dropped the luggage into the boot of the car. It was a lengthy drive into the company's offices and city showroom.

Hermann opened his office door, glad to be back in familiar territory. He walked to the sideboard next to his desk. He slid the bar fridge forward on running tracks and swung it to the right. Hermann spun the dials of the safe hidden behind the fridge and waited for the safe door to open. He placed the diamonds into a silk purse before laying this on the top shelf and closing the safe door.

The top drawer of his desk held the design the buyer had agreed on. Hermann extracted the design drawing and carried it in his left hand toward the showroom.

Normally the gold setting would have been prepared in advance of the stones arrival. Hermann was not keen to allow this though, because he was pretty sure the buyer was going to change his mind about the colour of the gold he wanted. Surprisingly this did not happen after all, and the buyer had confirmed his original choice of gold colour.

Hermann set his assistants to work to shape the first outline. The final details would be hand crafted to highlight the size and brilliance of the cut stone.

The work took several days until Hermann was finally satisfied that he had created an exquisite piece. He called the buyer late Thursday evening. "Yes, I understand," Hermann said. "I will catch the Friday-night red-eye and meet you at your office Saturday morning. Thank you."

Jean-Pierre had agreed to meet Hermann in Kuala Lumpur. He wanted to make sure his payment cleared the bank. While this annoyed Hermann, he agreed to it, if only to appease the Frenchman.

Hermann insisted that the payment would not be made until the gems were delivered to Beijing. Jean-Pierre accepted this and agreed to travel to Beijing with Hermann. They would meet at the Petronas Towers for the flight to Beijing. Hermann was able to schedule another client meeting for Friday afternoon that would take him to an early dinner after the meeting.

18

KUALA LUMPUR

Friday March 7, 2014

The Petronas Towers were a remarkable sight. Their height was only part of the attraction. The facade was equally impressive with its mountains of stainless steel and glass. The building shimmered in the late evening sunlight.

Hermann emerged from Tower One, leaving his appointment in Kuala Lumpur. His job took him all over the world, but Kuala Lumpur was still his favourite city. He approached the waiting driver, who opened the car door for him. He entered the familiar limousine ready for the trip to the airport.

The automatic doors of the Tower Shopping Complex slid open. Crowds constantly entered and left the vast retail area beneath the Petronas Towers. A tall, elegantly dressed gentleman appeared, walking toward the limousine.

Jean-Pierre climbed in on the other side of the vehicle and smiled at Hermann. Conversation would be limited while they could be overheard by the limo driver.

Arriving at the airport, the pair easily passed through customs and immigration inspections and wandered upstairs to the Malaysian Airlines business-class lounge.

Hermann settled in with his usual Scotch and a plate of the local chicken-satay sticks. Jean-Pierre ordered French champagne and fresh oysters.

They passed the time by checking e-mails, reading newspapers, watching the television news, and replenishing drinks from the bar. Some two hours later, the flight attendant approached them. "Mr. Wu, Mr. Claudens, your flight to Beijing has been called, if you would like to proceed to the gate now, please."

Hermann thanked her, collected his case, and touched his pocket as he stood up. With his vast treasure secure, Hermann strode away to the gate where his flight was boarding. Jean-Pierre was immediately behind him. He was not about to let Hermann out of his sight. There was a buyer in Beijing waiting for the Shwedagon Diamond. Payday loomed.

The announcement confirmed they were nearly ready to go. "This is the final call for all passengers on Malaysian Airways Flight MH370 for Beijing."

The Boeing 777 lifted off the runway on time at 12:40 a.m., Saturday, March 8.

Forty minutes later, as it prepared to enter Vietnamese air space, the last communication was made with Kuala Lumpur tower.

"Good night, Malaysian 370."

The jet's transponder went silent. Now unseen on the radar, the flight turned from its course directly north to make a sharp left turn and then vanished.

The next morning, the news bulletin flashed across the screen; the morning headlines were all focused on the missing plane. Associated Press reports:

"Malaysian Airlines flight MH370 left Kuala Lumpur heading for Beijing when it vanished from radar about an hour into the six hour flight. It is now believed to have crashed into the southern Indian Ocean with no survivors. Of the 239 people on board, 6 were Australians, 153 Chinese, with 1 Canadian, and 1 French national. No wreckage has been found. The search continues but everyone is puzzled as to how a plane bound to the north for Beijing could end up in an area off the coast of Kota Bharu, on Malaysia's east coast."

EPILOGUE—ANNIVERSARY

Experts have determined that one system on the missing jet could not be manually turned off. This system continued to ping the plane's flight path as it flew on into the night.

The plane is known to have flown for nearly eight hours after its last transmission. The search area has been moved south to the Australian coastline. Australian Defence Force teams were brought in to search the Indian Ocean west of the Australian coast. Malaysian teams working alongside the Aussies have been unable to locate the aircraft. The search area covered so far is in excess of sixty thousand square kilometres.

Early in the search, pieces of debris were found that were thought to have belonged to the missing flight. All of them have since been discounted as flotsam.

Nobody knows what happened to those on board. No wreckage has been found, no bodies recovered, and no personal possessions found floating in the ocean.

The Malaysian government has now formally declared the disappearance to be an accident. All on board are presumed dead.

Almost a year to the day of the disappearance of the airplane, a small package washes ashore on a beach south of Perth, the West Australian capital. It is a sealed cellophane packet containing plastic cutlery, salt-and-pepper sachets, and a paper napkin. Imprinted on the napkin is the logo of Malaysian Airlines. It is significant because it is sealed, and the contents are still intact.

No one can confirm what else was lost when the flight vanished off the radar, but the Shwedagon Diamond is missing, and there is one very angry media mogul in Beijing.

ABOUT THE AUTHOR

http://noleenjordan.com

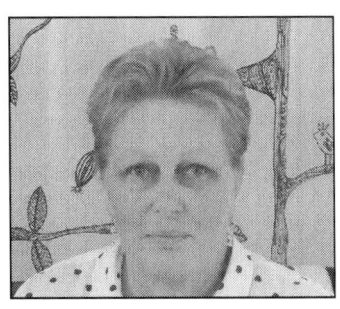 Retired from the corporate world, Noleen Jordan spent over twenty years in operations management and strategic sourcing in manufacturing, retail, and the entertainment industry. Her love of travel has given her many opportunities to experience other countries and cultures. Currently living in Sydney, Australia, with her husband, she is the mother of three and grandmother of six.

Printed in Great Britain
by Amazon